FIFTH INNING OFFICIAL

LINDA FAUSNET

My books contain steamy sex, bad words, and human beings of all sorts, include gay people. If you're not a fan of those things, you may want to stop reading now. If you're cool with that stuff, come take my hand and join me on this journey…

This book is a work of fiction. References to real people, events, establishments, organizations, or locales are intended only to provide a sense of authenticity and are used fictitiously. All other characters, and all incidents and dialogue, are drawn from the author's imagination and are not to be construed as real.

Published by Wannabe Pride 2023

Editing by Linda Hill

Cover Design by Chuck DeKett

FIRST EDITION.

❀ Created with Vellum

CAM

I *hate Baltimore.*

After a rough start to my season, the Atlanta Suns traded me. That was how I wound up in this dump. I knew I should have added a no-trade clause to my contract, but when you're trying to sign with a Major League Baseball team, you don't want to make any waves. And it's not like Atlanta was my dream city anyway.

No. That would be New York.

Born and raised in Brooklyn Heights, I grew up idolizing the New York Kings, and Kings Park was where I belonged. Not here.

I walked over to the bullpen to warm up, breathing in the fresh air of early May. Soon the humidity of summer would set in, but right now the weather was perfect. As I tossed a few warm-up pitches in the bullpen to my new catcher, Trace Ridgerton, even I had to admit Old Bay Stadium was beautiful. They say it's the most beautiful park in the majors. I adored Kings Park, but it was old as fuck and falling apart. Still, I hoped like hell they wouldn't tear it down and build a new one before I had the chance to play there as a King. As far as I was concerned, being a Baltimore Bay Bird was just another stop on my way to someday playing for New York.

"All right," Trace called over to me. "That's probably enough for now. Don't want to overdo it before the game."

I nodded, appreciating his concern. Trace seemed to be a good guy, and he knew his stuff. Though today would be our first official outing on the field, we'd gotten along well during practices. He liked my changeup pitch, as well as my slurve and fastball. He also thought I might be able to master a two-seamer fastball, but I wasn't quite so sure. Lots of pitchers knew how to toss a two-seamer—named that because you positioned your fingers on the seams at the top of the ball—but it worked best if you had excellent control. That took a lot of skill, and it was cool that Trace thought I could master it. And, bonus, the guy didn't hate me, which was more than I could say for the rest of the Bay Birds team.

It was probably my fault. I was super pissed about being traded and might have said so in the press, getting in a few digs at Baltimore in the process. I admit it wasn't cool, but it just slipped out. I was a lifelong Kings fan, and the Bay Birds were my mortal enemy. Though I always knew being traded was a possibility, I never dreamed I'd be wearing their tacky-ass orange and black uniform.

Still. I had a job to do. I was a major league pitcher, and my job was to kick ass, no matter what team I was playing for. Besides, I sure as hell had something to prove. I needed to make Atlanta regret throwing me away like a piece of garbage, and I needed to show the Kings I was worthy of playing for them.

Trace and I walked across the field toward the dugout together, but then he peeled off to visit with his girlfriend, Sarah. She also worked for the Bay Birds organization.

Something to do with charities and outreach and stuff. Trace and Sarah shared a two-year-old son, who he talked about all the time. I'd met Sarah briefly, and she seemed very sweet. Even though her job was to promote the Bay Birds and the city of Baltimore, she didn't appear to have any ill will toward me despite what I'd said in the press.

As I walked through the dugout and inside toward the clubhouse, I overheard my name, and the tone wasn't friendly. I stopped to listen before going in.

"Look, I get it, okay? He wants to play for New York because it's his hometown."

I was pretty sure that was Brady Keaton, our superstar shortstop.

"Nobody understands that more than me," he said, continuing his rant. "All I ever wanted to do was play for Baltimore, but I never trashed Boston or Richmond when I played for their teams.

"That's true," said some guy whose voice I didn't recognize.

"I mean, he's bitching about having to play for us," Brady grumbled. "But it's not like we're super thrilled to have him. One thing we need right now is solid, dependable starter pitching, and after those last few outings in Atlanta ..."

My blood boiled as I listened to my new teammate talking shit about me. I walked into the clubhouse quickly so there'd be no question that I'd overheard his rant.

"At least I didn't strike out and destroy my team's shot at the World Series," I snapped.

I regretted the words the instant they left my mouth.

It was like all the air had been sucked out of the room. Nobody said a thing.

Brady's unfortunate strikeout happened before he joined the Bay Birds, when he played for the Richmond

Dominoes. It was the kind of nightmare scenario every ballplayer feared, when the entire team's success or failure rested on your shoulders. You make the final out, and your team goes home instead of heading to the championship. It happens, and it really wasn't Brady's fault.

My harsh comment was way below the belt, especially since I barely knew the guy.

All eyes were on me as I headed over to my locker, so I got my shit together as quickly as I could. I knew I should apologize, but I just couldn't. I had too much pride. Instead, I shoved my bag into my locker and stalked out.

A stellar beginning for my first outing as a Baltimore Bay Bird.

Once I got out onto the mound, I did my best to focus on the task at hand. The very first batter hit a long fly ball that damn near made it out of the park. Thank God we had a good center fielder who nabbed it for the first out.

That was one hell of a wake-up call. I needed to settle the fuck down if I didn't want my pitching debut as a Bay Bird to be a totally humiliating disaster. After the way I acted earlier, even my teammates might want to see it happen.

I did settle down after the first inning, and things went more smoothly. The more I worked with Trace behind the plate, the more I trusted him. The guy had good instincts, and he called a good game. He seemed to have a feel for what my strongest pitch might be in any given moment. By the third inning I'd given up two runs. Not terrible, but not great either.

Then in the fifth inning I managed to load the bases. Though I understood his reasoning, it pissed me off when I saw Mick Edwards trudging toward the mound to yank me.

The large Friday night crowd didn't boo me when I left the field, but they didn't exactly cheer me either.

In New York, they'd have booed me for sure. Oddly, it made me miss my hometown more. Say what you will about New York fans, they didn't pull any punches. If you sucked, they let you know.

The relief pitcher only gave up one run, which I was responsible for since I let the guy get on base. In the end, the final score of the game was 5-4 with the Birds eking out a win. Not the greatest beginning for me, but it could have been worse.

It was early in the season, so I had time to get better. The Bay Birds had been steadily improving over the last few years, going from being perpetual losers to damn near making the playoffs last year. With any luck, I'd play a part in actually getting them there this year, showing New York and everybody else what I was made of.

After the game, I showered quickly, hoping to make a quick exit. On the way into the clubhouse I overheard yet another conversation about me. This time, though, it was a bit more encouraging.

"Cam's got a ton of potential, guys. I'm tellin' ya," Trace said in my defense. "And I'd rather he use it for us than Atlanta. He's got the stuff. I really believe that. He's not bad for a guy who rides a Harley."

I chuckled. Trace had shown me more pictures of his Indian motorcycle than he had of his kid.

When I walked into the locker room, the conversation ground to a halt. I got a few cool glances from the guys, but that was it. I'd made a pretty bad first impression, but I figured it would all blow over eventually. Like it or not, the Birds were stuck with me for a while, so they'd better get used to it.

I got dressed and headed out to the parking lot. Hopping on my Harley, I knew exactly what to do to pull myself out of my funk; head to the nearest bar, find the hottest woman there, and bang her senseless.

That never failed to do the trick.

2

WILDER

As I got ready to celebrate with my best friend at her bachelorette party, I couldn't help but wonder whether I would ever meet my Prince Charming. If it was going to happen, it probably wouldn't be tonight, considering we planned to take a stretch limo and go barhopping. There would be plenty of men out there all right, but the odds of finding a knight in shining armor at a Baltimore bar were pretty slim.

"You look gorgeous," I told Amanda, who was resplendent in her dark blue cocktail dress. Her eyes shone with joy, and she looked every bit the part of a happy bride-to-be. She glanced at herself in the mirror above the fireplace in her spacious living room, fluffing up her soft, wavy brown hair. I had helped her with her makeup and had found the perfect combination of eyeliner and eye shadow for her pretty brown eyes.

I couldn't have been happier for Amanda. We'd been best friends since grade school, and I loved her like a sister. I was beyond thrilled to be her maid of honor, especially since she had two biological sisters. And yet she and I were closer than they were.

I wandered over to the window to see if the limo had arrived yet. Thankfully, Amanda's fiancé was fairly wealthy and was bankrolling tonight's festivities. Broke as I was, I would have found a way to give my best girl a good send-off into married life somehow, but I was relieved I didn't have to. I'd already been working a ton of extra shifts at my bartending job lately, and yet it was still barely enough to cover the bills. Thank goodness I'd finally found a new roommate to help pay the rent. My old one suddenly dropped out of college, leaving me in the lurch financially when she moved out.

The car hadn't arrived yet, so I stood at the window for a moment, peering out at the acres of land on the property. Rusty and Amanda had recently bought this house in Hunt Valley, MD and had already started their new family, having adopted two adorable dogs. I smiled as I watched Lucky and Renner, a Chesapeake Bay retriever and a black lab respectively, joyfully roam around the property.

"I see the limo," I called to Amanda when I spotted the car in the distance.

"Okay, great!" Amanda called back. She rushed to the door to call the dogs into the house.

Gazing out at the stretch limo approaching, I felt like a lady-in-waiting on the way to the ball with the princess. Amanda's fiancé, Rusty, was certainly her Prince Charming. Their romance could have been right out of a fairy tale. Such a beautiful love story. Rusty had been the first baseman for the Baltimore Bay Birds, and Amanda had admired him from afar. She was a huge baseball fan, and he'd been her favorite player. Theirs had been a dramatic meeting for sure. Rusty had collapsed on the field during batting practice, and Amanda had bravely rushed onto the field and performed CPR on him, saving his life. They'd been together ever since.

Of course I was idealizing their situation. No relationship was perfect, and they'd had their ups and downs. Though Rusty had survived that terrifying medical emergency, it had spelled the end of his baseball career. Amanda had stood by him as he picked up the pieces of his broken dreams. Their love had been tested from the very beginning, yet it had strengthened their bond. This was a marriage that would truly last, and Amanda deserved no less.

"You okay?" Amanda asked with concern, walking over to where I stood at the window.

I'd failed to hide my feelings of sadness and, let's face it, jealousy over my best friend's happiness. I felt awful. The last thing I wanted was for my selfishness to put a damper on her special night.

"Yes! More than okay. I am so ready to party," I said with a smile.

She nodded slowly but she wasn't convinced. Amanda knew me better than anyone else in the world, and she could usually see right through me. I was a professional actress, or at least a wannabe one at the moment, but even that wasn't enough to fool her sometimes.

"I hope this isn't too hard for you," she said softly.

I swallowed against the lump in my throat. Amanda was the only person in the world who knew I'd had a broken engagement once. Well, the only one besides my horrid ex-fiancé. I caught Danny cheating literally the day he proposed, which I guess saved me the humiliation of having to tell everybody about our broken engagement. Still, you don't really get over something like that.

"Not at all," I insisted. "I am so happy for you, Amanda, and I can't wait to go out and celebrate!"

I *was* happy for her, but that didn't mean today would be easy. Naturally, attending a wedding would always remind me of what happened—or didn't happen—when it came to my own wedding. Danny and I were high school sweethearts, and our relationship had been about as cliched as they came. He was on the football team, and I was a cheerleader. Everybody thought we were so sweet together. We were "relationship goals," as they said. Our happy union was something people aspired to. After dating through most of high school, we went to different colleges but were both still here in Maryland. We didn't have to worry about a long-distance relationship, and everything had seemed perfect.

As I inwardly ruminated about Danny, I fussed with Amanda's hair, doing my best not to let on that I was starting to spiral into self-pity. It was hard not to sometimes. I lost my virginity to Danny, which made his betrayal even worse. We waited until we were eighteen. Well, *I* had waited. All that time I thought he was so wonderful and patient, waiting until I was ready. It wasn't until later I found out he'd cheated on me *a lot* during our time together. That made me feel so goddamned stupid. So gullible. I'd thought Danny and I were the envy of people everywhere, but I'd discovered at least some people knew different. I'd never know how many people were aware that Danny was unfaithful to me and yet nobody said a thing.

Despite the occasional moment of melancholy and self-pity, Amanda's wedding would be a good time. We were planning to pick up Amanda's sisters and some other friends, and we could drink as much as we liked and nobody had to drive anywhere.

Amanda and I started pre-gaming with champagne in

the limo, giggling like schoolgirls. I loved having a little time alone with her before we picked up the rest of the girls.

After we collected our friends Kellie and Lynn and Amanda's sisters, Penny and Cady, we headed over to a bar in Timonium for our first stop. I'd called all the bars on our list ahead of time to make sure it was okay to bring Cady, who was underage. Some places had rules about minors after 9pm, but I'd found a bunch of them that said it was cool as long as she didn't actually sit up at the bar.

The limo driver dropped us off right in front of CJ's Bar, helping each of us out of the back seat. It made me feel like I was stepping onto the red carpet of some fancy event. For a moment, I even allowed myself to pretend I was headed to the Tony Award ceremony where I'd been nominated for Best Actress in a Musical. The fantasy made me giggle, but it also sent a ripple of excitement through me.

It could happen someday. You never know.

Singing was the most important thing in my life, and it always thrilled me to daydream about performing for a living. Fantasizing about my future career was a hell of a lot more fun than wallowing in self-pity about Danny.

The moment I set foot in the bar, I got a lot of second glances from several men, but I tried to ignore them. More than anything, I wanted tonight's focus to be on Amanda. Not exactly the type to court attention, she wasn't comfortable wearing a bride-to-be crown. Much to my delight, she did consent to wearing a sash.

I handed Amanda's credit card to the bartender to start a tab. Though it was weird to use the guest of honor's credit card for her own celebration, Rusty had insisted on paying. We were afraid people might think I was using a stolen credit card if it had a dude's name on it. It was all the same money anyway, since Amanda and Rusty had a joint bank account, so she gave me her card for the night to avoid any awkwardness. I'd handle all the details, and she could just have fun.

I secured us a table in the back after we'd ordered our first round of drinks.

"This is so awesome," Cady gushed. Being too young to drink, barhopping was a new experience for her.

"Glad to have you with us," I said, clinking my beer glass with her soda. Both Penny and Cady had always looked up to their older sister, and they'd have a blast celebrating her tonight.

Damn, it felt good to be on the other side of the bar. I reveled in the luxury of not being the bartender for once. Though I didn't mind my bartending job, I certainly didn't want to be there forever.

"Here's to the beautiful and radiant bride!" I said, hoisting my drink as the others did the same.

"Thanks so much," Amanda said, blushing and smiling.

She looked so happy that my heart felt it could burst with joy. Since we were kids, we'd both dreamed of finding Mr. Right. Seeing her so excited about her future made it harder for me to feel sorry for myself and my own dismal love life. I couldn't wait to stand by her side and watch her marry the man of her dreams.

"Are you hungry?" I asked Amanda.

"Nah, I'm good for now. Will probably get something later."

"Anybody else want something to eat? Don't be shy. The groom said the sky's the limit," I said.

"Nice." Kellie smiled and reached for the menu.

"Order anything you like. The tab's in my name," I said, turning around to watch the live band play.

"Wilder, go dance," Amanda said. "You know you wanna."

"You sure?"

"Of course. Go have fun."

"Do you wanna come with me?" I asked her.

"Not now." She shrugged. "Maybe later."

I loved to dance, but Amanda was shyer and more inhibited. And yet, I refused to be the type to drag an unwilling person to the dance floor in the name of "fun." I'd never understood why people thought it was okay to force people out of their comfort zone by saying *It'll be fun* or *Don't be such a party pooper*. After she'd had a few drinks, Amanda might want to dance. And that was fine. But it was her choice.

"I'll go with you," Cady chirped excitedly.

"Awesome," I said. I liked this girl's enthusiasm.

Cady and I headed to the dance floor just as the band started playing one of my favorite songs.

"I love this song!" she said.

Laughing, I said, "I was about to say the same thing."

We danced together, having a great time. Until some drunk guy staggered up to me.

"Hey there, gorgeous," he said.

I stifled a groan. "Hi," I said to the guy, forcing a smile as I tried to move away from him. Fortunately, the dance floor was crowded enough that I was able to escape. For now.

I'd have to dig deep to find the strength to be polite to all the idiots who hit on me tonight. And there would likely be a lot. Not only was it annoying, it was quite depressing.

Because I knew a dirty little secret that I could never share with anyone, not even Amanda.

There's such a thing as being too beautiful.

There was simply no way to say that without sounding

like a stuck-up bitch, but it was the truth. People loved to quote the old song about learning the truth at seventeen that love was meant for beauty queens.

No. *Lust* was meant for beauty queens. Love was meant for average-looking girls like Amanda who could find a wonderful man who loved them for who they really were.

Since I was tall, blond, and had a good body, I turned heads everywhere I went. Men stared when I walked into a room and hit on me constantly, but they *never listened to a word I had to say.* They mostly stared at my boobs while they tried to figure out the right words to get me to go home with them. And sometimes, in a weak and lonely moment, I might actually do it. I nearly always regretted it, though. I loved sex and was certainly no prude, but I was tired of feeling used and hurt afterward. I wanted something *real.*

I considered myself an independent woman, so it wasn't like I needed a man. And yet I did want someone to share my life with. More and more lately, it seemed like that wasn't going to happen.

Cady and I managed to dance to one more song before that rando guy got near me again. He opened his mouth to talk, but I quickly bugged out of there.

"I'm gonna take a little break," I said to Cady.

She nodded, staying on the dance floor for the next song. I headed back to our table and slid down next to Amanda.

"Having fun?" I asked her.

She smiled and wrapped her arm around me. "Yes!"

"Good," I said, squeezing her back. "Let me know if you want to go to the next place or stay here or whatever. Your call."

"Okay, thanks. I'm good here for now," she said.

We'd put together a list of potential places to hit tonight.

That way if one place was a bust, we could always move on to the next. We figured we'd play it by ear and see how the night went, and we might end up hitting a bunch of places or stick with a place we liked. The only thing we knew for sure was that the last stop would be Power Bar and Grill, which her husband-to-be owned. Rusty was tending bar tonight, and I looked forward to delivering his bride to him after last call.

The bartender came over to me to take another round of drink orders rather than making me go over to the bar. I asked for another beer, and he checked on the rest of the table. It was especially nice not having to get up, since I was feeling relaxed and slightly buzzed.

"Hmmm, looks like Penny has a suitor," I said, nudging Amanda.

"Looks like," Amanda said with a smile as she watched a good-looking guy chatting up her sister at the other end of the table

"She broke up with what's-his-name, right?"

"Yeah, she did," Amanda said. "I'm glad. I never did like Ben very much."

The guy who was talking to Penny looked up when the bartender brought her drink. And that was when he saw me.

He stared in my direction, just like so many others had since I got here.

My heart sank. God, how I hated when some asshole ignored his date to look at me. It was incredibly disrespectful to the woman they were with, and it spoke volumes about the guy's character. No woman deserved to be treated like that. I saw the all-too-familiar look of hurt on Penny's face, and I wanted to slap the guy.

I turned away, hoping ignoring him would snap him

back to his senses and talk to the sweet girl he was sitting with instead of ogling me.

"So is Rusty gonna have a bachelor party?" I asked Amanda.

"Uh-huh. Next week. It's gonna be in West Virginia with some of his old friends. As much as he'd like to have some of his old Bay Bird teammates come along, it's just too hard with their baseball schedule. I'm just glad the guys can make it to the wedding."

"Yeah, that's most important," I said. Rusty and Amanda had planned their wedding for the Sunday night before Memorial Day. It would be after the Sunday ballgame. Most of their guests would have the day off the next day, and it wouldn't interfere with anyone attending remembrance ceremonies on actual Memorial Day.

I risked a glance over at Penny's guy. He was talking to her but still looking at me.

What a jerk.

Penny could do better, and I hoped she knew it.

Unfortunately, Amanda was no stranger to being treated the same way when she went out to bars with me. It hurt her feelings, and I despised it. I wished I could explain to other women that being stared at really wasn't the compliment they thought it was. After all, these strange men knew nothing about me. All they knew was that I was pretty. My looks weren't something I'd earned, so it wasn't like I was proud of my face and figure. And for all those guys knew, I could be a raging bitch. Or a hardened criminal. Sadly, some of them probably wouldn't have cared if I was. I was just arm candy. A bimbo to sleep with. Someone to show off to their friends.

I remembered when I first met Rusty. He could barely tear his gaze away from Amanda, and it was in that moment

I knew he was the one for her. He treated her like a princess, and I simply adored him for it. Rusty was well aware of the way Amanda had been treated in bars all these years, which was why he'd dropped to one knee and proposed in one. In front of a crowd of people, he'd professed his devotion to her and asked her to be his wife. I was honored to have been there to witness that beautiful moment. Rusty had made Amanda feel like the most beautiful and desired woman in the world, and she deserved no less.

I was lucky if a man remembered my name.

If only I could tell all those women who were envious of my looks that they had absolutely, positively, *nothing* to be jealous about.

CAM

I made the mistake of listening to the sports news while I rode my Harley toward Power Bar and Grill, where I hoped to pick up both a drink and a pretty girl for the night. The sportscasters mentioned my debut for the Bay Birds, of course, dissecting my performance in detail. It wasn't too bad, and they said I had potential. But then they went into a prolonged discussion about Brady Keaton, extolling his virtues in extensive detail. By the end of that news story, I felt like a complete and total jerk.

They talked about how Brady had been born and raised in Baltimore, and that becoming a Baltimore Bay Bird had been his lifelong dream. Naturally, I understood completely since I felt the same way about New York. Apparently, the guy donated tons of money to the city and did volunteer work with inner city youth in partnership with fellow Bay Bird Andre Jones. The radio featured several sound bites from Brady talking about how Baltimore certainly had its share of problems like poverty and drugs, but he wanted to do whatever he could to help his beloved city.

I sighed deeply as I steered my motorcycle into an Inner Harbor parking garage.

Yep. I was a total asshole today.

No wonder Brady was so upset with me, considering my initial remarks to the press about Baltimore included words like "cesspool" and "crack den." And then I'd made things so much worse by trashing his performance in the playoffs, which was rich considering I'd never even made it that far.

I'd always had the bad habit of blurting out what was on my mind without thinking it through. This time, I'd been lashing out because I was furious about being traded against my will, but that wasn't Brady's fault. I knew I had to apologize. Not just to mend fences with the team, but because it was the right thing to do.

As I walked the short distance from the parking lot to the bar, I looked out at the Chesapeake Bay. Sure, it was kinda polluted, but it wasn't like the Hudson River in New York was anything to brag about. The city lights made the water shimmer and the warm breeze helped calm my jangled nerves. Still, a drink or two would be even more helpful.

There was exactly one open seat at the crowded bar, so I quickly nabbed it. I looked around, taking in the cool baseball-themed bar with all the tables painted to look like baseballs and tons of signed player photos and other memorabilia on the walls. I'd been to plenty of sports bars, but I'd never heard of one that was exclusively devoted to baseball. I liked the vibe of this joint.

Two bartenders, one male and one female, were busily getting drinks for everybody. I waited for a minute or two before demanding attention from the tall redheaded dude.

Snapping my fingers, I said, "Need some service over here, ya dumb hick."

"Hold on," the guy said. "I'll be with you in a minute."

Then he poured a beer and brought it over to me, slamming it down on the bar top.

"On the house, ya stupid bastid," he said in a perfect imitation of my New York accent.

Chuckling, I slid the glass toward me. "How you been, man?"

Rusty grinned, blue eyes gleaming with mischief.

"Good. I'm doin' good." He glanced down the bar to see that the rush had died down a bit, so he turned back to me. "I wondered if you were ever gonna stop by and see me."

"Hey, I just got to Baltimore. Gimme a break," I told him, then took a swig of my beer.

"Yeah, you made quite an entrance when you blew into town," Rusty said with a raised eyebrow.

I winced. "I guess I did. I'm just so goddamn pissed off that Atlanta dumped me, and I guess I didn't handle it as well as I could have. Pretty sure the team hates me."

Rusty chuckled. "They'll come around. They're all good guys."

Looking around at the bar, I said, "So this is what you're doin' since you're too frail and delicate to handle baseball no more?"

"Yep," he said. "Can't play anymore, so now I own a place where I'm surrounded by a bunch of TVs where I can watch other guys livin' the dream."

Rusty smiled as he spoke, but I could hear the hint of sorrow in his voice. I couldn't imagine how hard it must have been to be forced out of baseball, but he was clearly doing well for himself. I first met him when we spent a summer in NYC on an amateur collegiate baseball team. We roomed together along with two other guys. You get to know each other real well under those circumstances. Since then, we'd seen each other a few times in the last couple of years when our teams had played each other.

"I hear some girl had to come rescue your bitch ass," I said bluntly.

We'd always busted each other's balls, so I figured I wouldn't insult him by pulling any punches.

Rusty couldn't hide the smile that reached all the way to his eyes. "Yep, she sure did."

I put a dramatic hand over my heart and quoted the news article headline: "'First she restarted his heart. Then she captured it forever.'"

Rusty cracked up. "Pretty much."

I knew damn well it wasn't just "some girl" who had saved his life. It had been all over the news that he was gonna marry that Ashley woman, or whatever her name was.

"Well, I'm so happy you've found the woman of your dreams," I said. The words came out sounding more sarcastic than I'd meant, but that was just my nature. I really was happy for the guy. "All I need right now is a decent hookup."

"Of course you do," he said with a grin.

"How's the action in here?" I asked, glancing around at the women in the joint.

"If I could answer that question, I wouldn't be getting married. How the hell should I know?"

"Fair point."

Rusty glanced over at the other bartender. She was getting a bit flustered with the latest rush of drink orders.

"Better get back to work here," he said.

"You'd better. I hear the owner's a real dick."

"Oh, you!" Rusty said with an exaggerated wave of his hand in my direction, making me laugh. It was good catching up with my old buddy, and I was glad to see he hadn't lost his sense of humor.

Scanning the room, I saw a number of potential bedmates for the night. In particular, I had my eye on an attractive brunette at the other end of the bar. She didn't seem to have a man with her, and she was in the perfect strategic location to make eye contact. I was totally locked on to her.

That was until a bachelorette party walked in.

Hot damn. The tall blond woman with the maid of honor sash was a fucking knockout. Sorry, Ms. Brunette. We have a better contender here.

This girl was incredible. Seriously, she could have been a supermodel with her big boobs, tiny waist, and long legs. She had piercing blue-green eyes that I could see shining from all the way across the room. I watched her for a few minutes while she led the group of female revelers over to a table that was big enough for all of them.

Rusty came over and swapped out my empty beer glass for a full one.

"I see a whole bunch of pretty girls just came in," I said, gesturing toward the bachelorette party in the back.

"The bride is the prettiest," Rusty said.

I shrugged. "If you say so."

He turned to look at me, narrowing his eyes in disapproval at my remark. It took me a few seconds to register the problem.

"Oh," I said. "I mean, she is pretty and all. Very pretty. Beautiful in fact."

Rusty laughed and shook his head, enjoying the show of watching me struggle to remove my foot from my mouth.

Upon closer inspection, she was kinda cute with her wavy brown hair and gentle brown eyes. She was one of those girls you knew was a nice person just by looking at her.

"That tiny thing saved your life?" I asked, marveling at how petite she was.

"I know, isn't that crazy?" Rusty said, gazing at her with amazement.

"So, since the loveliest woman over there is already taken ... What's the story with the maid of honor?"

Eyeing me with suspicion, he said, "She's single. But she's Amanda's best friend, so don't--"

Rusty got distracted when his bride-to-be approached the bar. I didn't even have to turn my head to know what he was looking at. I could see it in his face. My old buddy was clearly head over heels in love with her, and he did look at her as if he thought she was the most beautiful woman in the world.

"Hey, beautiful," he said, leaning over the bar to kiss her. "You guys having fun?"

"We really are," she said, her eyes shining with happiness.

"Good. Amanda, I want you to meet an old friend of mine."

Amanda. That was her name. I knew it started with an "A." She turned toward me and her eyes lit up with recognition.

"Camden Becker!" she exclaimed. I was surprised she knew my name. For one horrible moment, I was afraid maybe I'd slept with her at some point and just didn't remember. "You're the new starting pitcher for the Baltimore Bay Birds."

Relief swept through me. I should have realized how unlikely it was that I'd slept with her. She lived in Baltimore, and I didn't get around quite *that* much.

"Amanda's a huge baseball fan," Rusty said proudly. "She probably knows as much about it as me, if not more."

"Lucky thing for you, huh?" I said, and he nodded. "Nice to meet you, Amanda."

"You too," she said. Glancing up at one of the sports televisions, she asked, "Didn't you pitch tonight?"

"Sure did."

"I thought that was you. I wasn't paying as much attention to the game as I normally do." Amanda tugged at her bride-to-be sash as if to explain. "But I saw a little bit of it. You looked pretty good out there."

"Thanks," I said, tipping my beer mug in her direction. Yep, she did seem like a nice girl. Good for Rusty.

Amanda gazed at him with the same expression of adoration that he'd had for her. Even a cynic like me couldn't help but be touched by their love story. Rusty could have been dead if it hadn't been for her, and now they were gonna spend the rest of their lives together. That was pretty cool.

"Oh, Cam," she said. "You should come to the wedding!"

"That would be great," Rusty said with a smile.

"I don't want to impose," I said. "It's coming up pretty soon, isn't it?"

"Memorial Day Weekend," Amanda said. "But I haven't sent the final head count to the caterer. It would be no problem, really. We'd love to have you. Most of the rest of the team will be there."

Oof. I understood why Amanda thought that would be a selling point, but I wasn't exactly the most popular guy on the Bay Birds. Still, I wanted to be there for my friend.

"That would be great, Amanda. Thanks so much," I told her.

"Perfect! Let Rusty know if you'd like a plus one. Just need to know by next week."

Amanda blew Rusty a kiss before heading back to her table.

I would not require a plus one—weddings were the perfect place to pick up women when you went stag. Glancing over at the sexy maid of honor, I knew I wouldn't try to take her home tonight. The last thing I wanted to do was break up Amanda's party, since it was her special night.

The wedding, however, would be a perfect time to make my move on her best friend.

4

WILDER

At last, it was the morning of Amanda and Rusty's big day. I was gonna meet up with her at her house with the rest of the bridal party for mimosas and to get our hair and makeup done.

"Okay, I'm heading out," I said to my roommate as I walked into the living room of the rowhouse we shared in downtown Baltimore.

"Oh yeah, today's the wedding, right?" Kerry asked me, looking up from where she lay on the couch reading a book about art history.

Not only was Kerry Jordan beautiful with her dark black skin and soulful, dark brown eyes, but she was amazingly talented. As a student at the Maryland Institute College of Art, or MICA, she created the most incredible sculptures. Her specialty was sculpting animals—we had some gorgeous lion and gazelle sculptures in our otherwise humble living room. We didn't have much else since we were basically starving artists.

"Yup," I said.

"That's cool. Hope you have fun," she said with a smile.

"Thanks." Kerry and I hadn't known each other long, but I really liked her. We met through a mutual friend who knew we were both in need of a roommate.

Since the ceremony wasn't until later this evening, the bridal party had plenty of time to get ready. That made for a leisurely morning, especially since Amanda wasn't a bridezilla. Since the bride generally set the tone for the day, her easygoing manner made it clear she just wanted today to be fun. I served as bartender for the celebratory mimosas we sipped while getting our hair and makeup done.

Rusty once again arranged for a luxurious stretch limo for us. This time, it would take us to the church. As with the bachelorette party, me and the other bridesmaids had a wonderful time together as we celebrated Amanda on her big day. Before we knew it, it was time for the wedding ceremony.

We stood together at the back of the church with gentle organ music as the soundtrack for this tender moment.

After more than a year of planning, not to mention a lifetime of dreaming, at last it was time for Amanda to walk down the aisle.

"It's finally happening," I said to her as I blinked away my tears.

"I know," Amanda whispered. "Can you believe it?"

My best girl was absolutely stunning in her white beaded gown lined with delicate white roses. Her makeup was flawless, highlighting the richness of her brown eyes, and her brown hair was curled in perfect ringlets falling past her shoulders. Best of all was her radiantly shining face.

A wave of childhood memories overloaded my emotions as I remembered the two of us as little girls dreaming about our wedding days. And now the fantasy was becoming a reality. For one of us, anyway.

"Just like we always dreamed of," I said, my voice practically a whisper.

"I know," Amanda said, visibly fighting tears.

My mind couldn't help flashing back to Danny. Our engagement may have lasted for fewer than twenty-four hours, but I'd spent years prior dreaming about marrying him. As we danced together at the prom, I had fantasized about someday dancing at our wedding. I swallowed hard, trying to squash those painful memories. After all, today was *so not about me.*

"And you know what the best part is?" I asked as I straightened her delicate veil. "I have absolutely no doubt whatsoever that Rusty is the one for you." I might have totally misjudged Danny, but somehow I just knew Rusty was different.

"Me neither," she said, the tears finally spilling over.

"No, don't do that! You'll mess up your makeup."

"I know, I know," Amanda said, and then carefully dabbed at her eyes with her pinky fingers.

The processional music started up and she let out an excited squeal.

"It's time," she said, eyes shimmering with happiness.

Amanda's sisters processed down the aisle first, and then it was my turn as maid of honor. A brief but intense wave of sadness washed over me as I walked the white carpet toward the altar. It had been almost two years since my engagement was called off, but it still hurt. At least I could take solace in the fact that the bride herself was the only one in attendance who knew what had happened with Danny. Pitying looks from the congregation for the poor, jilted maid of honor would have been awful.

I took a deep, cleansing breath and smiled. At first, I had to draw upon all my acting expertise to appear happy, but I quickly found my dark feelings fading away as I thought about why I was here. Supporting my best friend on her special day truly was an honor, and I was deeply, genuinely happy for her.

Taking my place at the front of the church, I turned to see Amanda processing down the aisle. As stunning as she looked walking arm in arm with her father, I tore my attention from her so I could see Rusty. Wedding guests always watch the bride at this point of the ceremony, but I always loved watching the groom.

Rusty was positively transfixed by his soon-to-be wife. His deep blue eyes opened wide as if wanting to take in every inch of his beautiful bride.

That's it right there. That's The Look.

After my disastrous engagement, I promised myself the only way I would ever even consider getting married was if a guy looked at me like that. The Look was how you knew a man was your soulmate. When he looked at you like you were the only woman in the world. It was hard to put into words exactly what The Look, well, *looked* like, but I always knew it when I saw it. A tender expression of utter love and devotion that was reserved for only one person.

The Look that meant he would never cheat on you.

I was lucky if a guy looked me in the eye at all. They were usually focused on the rest of my body.

With a sharp shake of my head, I forced myself to stop with the damned self-pity already. Amanda had found the perfect husband, and that was all that mattered to me. It was unlike me to be so focused on my love life. Only in the last few weeks had I been hyper-focused on the wedding. Once the wedding and reception were over, I could shift my concentration back on other things in life. Namely, my singing and acting career. I didn't even have to wait—I was scheduled to sing at the reception. As always, I knew the moment I began singing everything would feel right again. I didn't need a man to complete me. Singing always soothed my soul, and nobody could take that away from me.

Once Amanda reached the front of the altar and took her place beside Rusty, he caught my eye and smiled. I could feel the happiness emanating from him, and a renewed surge of joy flooded my body. That was the beauty of happiness stemming from love. It was contagious.

What a privilege it was to be here beside them today.

I watched the lovely wedding ceremony as Amanda and Rusty vowed to be together until death did they part. Those words had special meaning, considering the fact that Amanda had saved his life on the day they met. To think, Rusty had barely survived that awful day, and now he was getting married. I choked up as I watched him pledge his love to my best friend. Amanda and I were practically sisters, and I simply adored my new honorary brother-in-law.

After the ceremony, the bridal party did the obligatory photo shoot at the altar and took a few pictures outside the church. The breeze whipped our carefully styled hairdos around, making us laugh as we tried to protect our looks. A sense of warmth and happiness enveloped me as I stood with Amanda's sisters and her parents. I was practically a part of their family, considering how many sleepovers Amanda and I had shared over the years.

With the photos taken, we were finally released to head over to the reception, which was being held at a fancy hotel in downtown Baltimore.

Wedding receptions were often full of single guys

hoping to score with a bridesmaid. Lucky for me, I was able to process into the reception on the arm of Rusty's best man, a close friend of his since childhood. Charlie was a perfect gentleman, and he had a date to the wedding. It was a relief to be paired up with a man who was already spoken for, so there was no pressure or awkwardness.

Rusty's other groomsmen included another friend from his hometown of West Virginia and Brady Keaton, superstar shortstop of the Bay Birds. Both of those men were happily married, so there was nothing to worry about there either.

After giving the guests enough time to help themselves to drinks and appetizers, it was time for the toasts. Once again, Charlie proved to be a perfect gentleman, telling funny stories about Rusty, but nothing raunchy or inappropriate. He expressed his happiness and best wishes for his good friend and his new bride via a speech that was short and sweet.

Then it was my turn to speak. As a performer, public speaking was not a problem for me. And, as with being in the wedding, I considered it my privilege to toast the happy couple.

"Amanda and I have been best friends since we were little girls," I began. "And, like many little girls, we often dreamed about our wedding days and we fantasized about the type of man we would marry. As I stand here today, I can state with confidence that Rusty has surpassed even our fondest girlhood fantasies."

As a fair-skinned, redheaded man, it was impossible to miss the incredibly endearing blush on Rusty's face.

"We all know Rusty's terrifying medical emergency is what first brought these two together," I continued. "They've endured a lot since then. Sadly, on that terrible, frightening day, a very special dream of Rusty's died."

Though I didn't want to be a downer on this happy day, I felt it was important to acknowledge the couple's strength and courage in facing tough times together. After all, that was what marriage was all about.

"But that same day, a new dream began. And now we are all gathered together to celebrate that dream."

I saw Amanda wipe away a tear and I had to struggle to hold my emotions in check.

"I've always felt that one of the most important keys to a healthy relationship is the ability to fight fair. I think anyone who knows Amanda knows she is the queen of conflict resolution."

Gentle laughter from the crowd affirmed my statement.

"I remember when we were on the playground in grade school, two girls started fighting. And I mean, *girl* fighting. Screaming, hair-pulling, the works. To this day, I have no idea what little Amanda said to them, but before the teacher could even reach them, my girl had those two sitting together and hashing out their feelings like they were in a psychiatrist's office. I've even seen her sit her two dogs down together when *they* aren't getting along."

More warm laughter emanated from the crowd.

"Because of this, I have no doubt that she will be able to keep Rusty in line, not to mention any kids they might have. But really, anyone who has seen the two of them together can tell that they will always fight fair, because they not only have deep love for each other, but also deep respect. Amanda and Rusty, your relationship began with sickness, but now I wish you nothing but health and happiness from this day forward. Marriage is for better or for worse. You started off with the worst, and you weathered that terrible storm together. And now," I said, raising my glass and encouraging the other guests to do the same, "let us wish you both the best that life has to offer. To Rusty and Amanda Power!"

My tears spilled as I lifted my glass to my lips. Cheers and well wishes erupted from around the room, and I could feel the warm love of the couple's family and friends.

After the toasts, we all settled down to enjoy a delicious dinner. I was grateful to have a chance to sit and relax for a while. Soon enough, it was time for the bride and the groom to share their first dance. Like me, Amanda was a big Disney and Broadway fan, so many of this evening's selections came from different movies and shows. She had chosen "I See the Light" from the Disney movie *Tangled.* Such a beautiful choice, and I loved the way the lyrics reminded me of how Rusty had emerged from the darkness and found the light with his soulmate.

The guests all gathered around in a circle, surrounding the couple as they danced. My emotions were running high again, just as they had when I'd walked down the aisle in the church. As I watched Amanda and Rusty dance together with their arms wrapped lovingly around each other, it felt like my own prince was a million miles away. Times like this, I wondered if he even existed.

I wasn't the only one caught up in this deeply poignant moment. Rusty's poor mother was a mess. The petite lady with the reddish-gray hair leaned against her husband and wept as she watched her son dance with his new wife. That dear woman had come so close to losing her baby. Amanda told me Rusty's mom had actually screamed with excitement when she found out the woman who'd saved his life was going to be her daughter-in-law.

Amanda caught sight of her new mother-in-law and motioned her over to join the dance. There wasn't a dry eye in the house after that happened.

I suddenly felt wrung out, exhausted by the emotions of the day, so I sat at a nearby table. I needed to gather my strength, since I was supposed to sing soon.

"Hey there," came a female voice from just above me. I looked up to see Julia Frederick. She was the head groundskeeper of Old Bay Stadium and was married to Bay Bird second baseman Matt Jovey. Julia was a good friend of Amanda's, so I'd hung out with her a few times. She was always fun to be around.

Julia took a seat next to me as we watched the end of Amanda's dance with her new husband and mother-in-law. Another slow romantic song started up, and I turned away.

"If you don't mind my saying," Julia began, "I know weddings can kinda suck when you're single."

I laughed. "Is it that obvious?"

I hated being the cliched lonely bridesmaid, but that was me.

"Only because I've been there," Julia said with deep kindness in her pretty hazel eyes. "I was a bridesmaid in Lyric's wedding like *right after* my fiancé dumped me."

"Oh, shit," I blurted out in shock, making her laugh.

"Yeah. It was pretty awful."

"I can't imagine how hard that must have been." Even after all this time, it was still hard to attend weddings. I couldn't fathom having to go to one when the pain was still raw.

"Oh, I was a hot mess. I tried to hide it for Lyric's sake, of course."

"Yeah," I said quietly. "Amanda's my best friend, so ..."

Julia nodded in understanding. She was a pretty girl with a sweet and vivacious personality. What kind of idiot would have broken an engagement with her? Though I felt terribly guilty about it, it was comforting to know I wasn't the only one here who'd lost a fiancé. If that could happen to an amazing woman like Julia, it could happen to anyone. And that things had turned out wonderfully for her in the long run, I was truly grateful. She deserved a happy ending.

"For what it's worth," she said, "the very next wedding I attended after Lyric's was my own. So you just never know when you'll meet the right guy."

I nodded, wishing I could believe her.

"Guys don't come any classier than Matt," I said, enjoying the smile that broke out on her face at the mere mention of her husband. "His on-field proposal was like something out of the movies."

"Right?" Julia exclaimed. "It was so totally unexpected. And Matt's usually pretty quiet and reserved, you know? For him to get out there and get down on one knee in front of all those people ... I'll never know where he found the courage. But he knew how much Old Bay Stadium means to both of us, and that's what made it so perfect."

I sighed dreamily. It truly was perfect.

I glanced back at the dance floor just in time to see Rusty dip Amanda. It was adorable. Then he pulled her back up into his arms, gazing into her eyes. And there it was again.

The Look.

I made the mistake of looking around the ballroom and caught sight of no fewer than three men staring directly at my tits. I turned away in disgust.

"You all right?" Julia asked, her brow furrowed with concern.

"Yes," I said with sudden confidence and conviction in my voice. "I admit it's kinda hard to see the bride and groom so happy when I don't have anybody like that in my life, but if nothing else, it convinces me to never, ever settle. I'm gonna wait for my handsome prince. And if he never shows up, then I'm gonna find my happily ever after on my own."

"Good for you!" Julia said, slapping her hand down on the table and rattling the champagne glasses.

I laughed. "Thanks, girl."

Okay. Enough of the self-pity.

A renewed surge of energy flowed through me knowing I would get up and sing for the crowd soon. That was where I really shone; that was my happy place. Performing was incredibly healing to my soul.

Forget finding a man.

In a few moments, it would be just me and the music.

5

CAM

Ah, damn.

So much for my plan to pounce on Wilder at Rusty's wedding reception.

I'd gotten a front-row seat while she talked with Julia Frederick. The two of them were so lost in conversation, they didn't even notice when I sat down at the table. Damn, that Wilder was one fine-ass looking woman. Especially in a bridesmaid gown that would have been so much fun to rip off her in a fit of passion. I loved a girl with long hair, and those blond curls cascading down her back were gorgeous. My balls ached just thinking of how hot her messy, post-sex hair would look after I rocked her world for a few hours.

But it was never gonna happen.

The sexy maid of honor was on the hunt for something real. A boyfriend, and eventually a husband. That was the last damn thing I wanted. I refused to be tied down, which was why I'd never had a steady girlfriend.

Wilder was lonely and hurting, making her easy prey. And that was precisely why I had no choice but to leave her the hell alone. I was not about to screw around with somebody's heart just to get laid. Instead, I scanned the room to see if I could find a decent hookup for the night. What I needed was a girl just looking for a good time like I was.

As I searched the dance floor for possible bedmates, my eyes landed on the bride and groom. They did look pretty cute together, I'd give them that. There were lots of gorgeous women here tonight, and yet Rusty could barely keep his eyes off Amanda. It was such a foreign concept to me, the idea of being with one woman for the rest of your life. Just bizarre. Marriage seemed so outdated to me. What was the point?

My parents hated each other. When I was growing up, most of my friends had parents who hated each other. Some got divorced while others toughed it out. Either way, it didn't look like much fun to me. I was perfectly happy in my bachelor pad all by my lonesome, thank you very much.

The DJ stopped the music to make an announcement, and I wondered if it was time to cut the cake already. Instead, he said the maid of honor was going to sing a song for the bride and groom to dance to.

Sweet.

I still had no intentions of making a move on Wilder, but that didn't mean I couldn't enjoy the view of her. With her at the microphone for a few minutes, I could stare at her all I wanted. That would give me time to memorize her curves for use later when I needed a little solo sexual relief.

Damn, she really is a knockout.

Wilder strode up to the microphone like a pro, and her confidence was such a turn on. I saw fire in her eyes.

Never mind her eyes. I zeroed in on those luscious tits of hers, and I wished I could take a picture of them. Not that I would forget them any time soon.

Pausing a moment to give everyone a chance to settle

down and listen, Wilder surveyed the audience. She had a commanding presence, and people shut up pretty quickly once they saw her standing up there. The music started up, and Wilder began to sing. I recognized the song immediately. "All I Ask of You" from *The Phantom of the Opera*. I was no fan of showtunes, but I lived in New York and the song was goddamn everywhere. Even though the show had closed after a thirty-five-year run, people were still obsessed with it.

A shiver went through me when I heard her voice, and somehow I forgot all about her tits. For the first time, I looked at her face. And I mean *really* looked at her, and I was mesmerized by what I saw.

Gone was the lonely bridesmaid longing for love. In her place was a woman with fiery passion who sang with the power and beauty of a Broadway star. Her performance was much more than just a maid of honor singing at her friend's wedding. Wilder was the real deal.

I listened to her rich, golden voice and watched her face transform from being a dateless wedding attendant to a woman who was deeply and unabashedly in love.

For one crazy moment I imagined she was singing about me.

I literally shook my head as it to rid myself of such romantic nonsense.

Where the hell did that come from?

Clearly, Wilder was as good an actress as she was a singer. And that was really saying something with those pipes. I tore my gaze away from her for just a moment to see if everyone else in attendance was as transfixed as I was by Wilder's performance.

And the answer was yes.

Nobody moved. The catering staff had stopped gathering dishes, and wedding guests were either frozen in place with drinks in their hands or seated motionless at the tables. Everyone stared at Wilder as if relishing every sweet note of her song.

Amanda listened with rapt attention, her hand over her heart as she gazed lovingly at her friend. What a doll she was. She must have known having Wilder sing would take the attention away from her, the bride, on her special day. She obviously didn't care. There was no jealousy on her face, only pride. I couldn't help smiling. Rusty had chosen wisely. Amanda had a heart of gold.

Not wanting to miss another second of Wilder's performance, I turned back to her.

She was looking directly at me. A sharp bolt of electricity rocketed through my body when our eyes connected. For a brief second, it felt like she really was in love with me. Impossible, since we'd never even met. Before I knew it, Wilder turned and gazed at some other random guy. I guess that was what great performers did. Made each member of the audience feel like a part of the show, if only for a few seconds.

All too soon, the song was over. Everybody went nuts, clapping, cheering, and whistling. Wilder smiled sweetly at her adoring audience, then she stepped away from the microphone. Amanda rushed over to pull her into an embrace.

I sat in a daze, still feeling as if I'd been hit by lightning. I wasn't sure why I was so blown away by Wilder's performance. I'd heard tons of good singers before. I'd been to more Broadway shows than I cared to admit, mostly when I was dragged there by friends and relatives who lived out of town. Some shows were great, some not so much. But I'd never reacted to any performance like this. Something about the way that girl sang, how she put her entire self into it, just struck me as incredible.

I recognized passion when I saw it, and it occurred to me that Wilder felt the same way about performing as I did when I pitched. Not something you can really explain, but when you're in the zone like that, everything else just falls away. Nothing else matters.

For the rest of the reception, I stared at Wilder as much as I could get away with it. Not that she would have noticed, considering she spent the rest of the party fending off various men who kept hitting on her. I admired her resolve. She clearly meant it when she'd said she was waiting around for Mr. Right. Good for her.

At least that was what I told myself. That I was glad she wasn't going home with any random guy because she deserved better. While it might be true, really the thought of her going home with another guy made me crazy.

I was so obsessed over the gorgeous maid of honor that I completely lost track of time. It wasn't until the reception was over and the place was nearly empty that I realized I'd forgotten to pick up a girl to take home for the night.

Damn.

Well that's a first.

6

―――――――

WILDER

I felt like a different woman after I sang, just like I knew I would. Well, not a different woman exactly. Singing made me feel more like myself again. Being at my best friend's wedding had dredged up so many painful memories of my broken engagement, but the pain vanished into thin air once I took to the stage. With adrenaline coursing through my veins, I was back in control again. Performing was my happy place and an excellent reminder of why I didn't need a man to complete me. Finding my prince would be wonderful, but it certainly wasn't a necessity. Singing also reminded me I had no intention of being a bartender forever.

Amanda gave me a huge hug after I sang. With tears in her eyes, she said, "Thank you so much. That was incredible. Just like we always dreamed."

"I know," I said quietly in her ear as we embraced. Ever since I found my calling as a singer when I was a little girl, we'd agreed I would someday sing on her wedding day. And that beautiful day had finally arrived.

A bunch of guys hit on me after I sang, which I guess I

should have taken as a compliment. But it didn't really feel like it. Being onstage simply brought me to their attention. As usual, their eyes roamed around my body as they spoke to me. And, as usual, they weren't listening to a word I said. Any guy who wanted to be with me would have to understand, really *understand* my hopes and dreams of being on Broadway. Simply tolerating me when I talked about it wasn't enough.

"I'm not looking for a relationship right now" was my standard response to the randos who tried incessantly to chat me up. "Tonight I just wanna be here for Amanda."

Sometimes I felt bad about being so dismissive, but I'd had enough experience to know when a guy was just trying to get me into bed. Barely looking me in the eye was my first clue. The second was that bored look when I spoke.

Finally, a truly decent man with nothing but good intentions walked up to me.

"That was so beautiful, Wilder," Rusty said, his blue eyes shining with gratitude. "Thank you so much."

He engulfed me in a big bear hug, which was exactly what I needed.

"You're so welcome," I said.

Being around Rusty boosted my spirits even more. That man exuded positive energy, a true testament to his resilience, given everything he'd been through. He was a reminder that there were still great guys out there.

I enjoyed the rest of the reception immensely. Singing gave me a natural high as always, and putting away a few glasses of wine didn't hurt either. While Amanda was busy dancing with her new husband, I spent the rest of the party giggling with Julia, Lyric, Sarah, and Amanda's sisters.

They announced last call at the bar, and then it was time for Amanda and Rusty to take the floor for their last dance. I watched the groom take his bride's hand, tenderly leading the way. Amanda's delicate bridal gown swished with her graceful movements, and the two of them looked like something out of a fairy tale.

A sharp stab of pain pierced my heart as I remembered how my would-be groom wound up screwing another woman less than twenty-four hours after proposing to me. Tears pricked my eyes.

Goddammit.

Just when I thought I was okay. A few minutes ago I'd been having a great time, and now I felt as if the wind had been knocked out of me.

I couldn't take my eyes off the two of them, swaying together to the music. There it was once again.

The Look.

Rusty gazed into Amanda's eyes as if he were gazing directly into her soul.

I couldn't help wondering if any man would ever see me as anything more than a trophy.

Wiping my eyes, I hoped if anyone saw me they would mistake my tears as ones of joy for my friend and not what they really were. Tears from the Land of Self Pity.

Blechhh. I berated myself for being so pathetic. And yet, weddings were always emotional for people, and anyone who'd suffered a bad breakup would feel the same way I did. Tomorrow, in the light of day, I could hopefully get back to feeling more like myself. Even singing all alone at the top of my lungs had a way of making me feel better.

When the romantic song finally ended, I put on my best actress face so I could say goodbye to the happy couple before they retired to their hotel room. Tomorrow, they would leave for their honeymoon in Hawaii.

More tears and hugs from Amanda. We had shared so

many today, and yet each time was meaningful. I loved that girl so damn much.

"Thank you for making my wedding so perfect. I couldn't have asked for a better maid of honor."

"I'm so, so happy for you," I told her for the millionth time today. And those words, too, were meaningful every time. I was overjoyed for my best friend.

I hugged Rusty one more time as well. Then I jokingly punched him on the shoulder and asked lightly, "So you think I'll ever find the perfect guy for me?"

He took the question much more seriously than I'd expected. Rusty gazed at me for a moment and then gently brushed my hair away from my face. "I hope so, Wilder. You deserve it. You really do."

My breath caught in my throat as I looked into Rusty's caring blue eyes. He'd seen through my brave face and saw my pain.

And he cared.

"Thank you," I said, fighting tears as I pulled him in for another much-needed hug.

7

CAM

I got home late and in a foul mood. How could I have gotten so distracted that I literally *forgot* to secure a hookup for tonight? Weddings are usually the easiest place to pick up girls, especially when you were a semi-famous pro athlete. I couldn't believe I blew it. It would have been the perfect time to talk to the ladies, considering most of the guys on the team barely acknowledged my presence. Trace had been cordial enough, but everyone else ignored me. It was all my fault, but it sucked.

I still couldn't get Wilder out of my head. A little part of me regretted not going for it with her, but it wouldn't have been right. As confident as I was in my bedroom skills, no matter how great the sex, she would have regretted it in the morning. She'd said she was waiting for her "handsome prince," and that was definitely not me.

Grumbling out loud with frustration, I pounded a few whiskeys back and then I hit the sack. The sooner the day was over, the better.

I SLEPT in the next morning since the game didn't start until 4:35. I wasn't pitching, but I still had to show up and be in uniform with the team. I felt slightly better after getting a good night's sleep. *Slightly.*

With the coffee brewing, I puttered around my stupid rented apartment. Still, I was lucky to not only be able to afford a nice place, but also that I'd found a luxury apartment on such short notice. It wasn't like the Atlanta Suns had given me a lot of warning before cutting me loose.

Bastards.

And yet I understood I was at least partly to blame for what had happened with them. Once again, my big mouth had gotten me in trouble. I couldn't help it. I was mad because I'd been pulled off the mound in the third inning. In retrospect, I shouldn't have said I'd seen better managers at McDonald's.

Once the coffee was ready, I poured a cup and took the steaming mug out with me to the balcony. Such a nice view. Too bad it was a view of a city I hated. Somehow, I had to keep my resentment in check because I could not afford any more media missteps. Trashing the city I played for wasn't going to win me any fans here. Not that I cared much about popularity, but I needed to prove I was a good pitcher if I ever wanted to get the hell out of here and play for New York, where I belonged.

My stomach grumbled, sounding as cranky as I was. I toasted a couple of Pop Tarts to tide me over until lunchtime when I would eat something healthier and more substantial before the game. I settled in front of my computer at my desk in the living room to browse the internet while I ate.

I resisted temptation as long as I could, but I soon found myself typing "Wilder Price" into the search engine. A *ton* of results came up. There were lots of professional photos of her looking even more alluring than she had last night. She exuded confidence in the pictures, like while she was on the stage as opposed to the quieter moments when she sat by herself at the reception. I also found a whole bunch of videos of her singing.

Some of the songs were from newer musicals. Ones that I had heard of or had seen billboards for in New York but that I wasn't familiar with. Wilder sang the hell out of some song called "Let Me Be Your Star." It was a showstopper of a song, and she really belted it out, showing her incredible range. In another video, she was singing the classic song "Anything Goes" from I forget what musical. She also performed a bunch of Disney songs, like from *Beauty and the Beast* or *The Little Mermaid* or some shit.

Watching those videos was addicting. I felt the same chills of delight as I had seeing her perform last night. I couldn't take my eyes off her; something about her was so mesmerizing. And that voice ... so beautifully feminine, yet strong and powerful. Her rendition of "On My Own," that famous song about unrequited love from *Les Miserables* was particularly lovely and intense.

Holy fuck.

Two hours had passed since I started down the Wilder Price rabbit hole, and I hadn't even finished watching all the videos she'd uploaded.

I probably wouldn't have noticed the time if my stomach hadn't started rumbling. Forcing myself to step away from the computer, I got up in sort of a daze. I had that odd kind of hazy, dreamy feeling you got sometimes after seeing a particularly powerful movie.

I started second-guessing my decision not to shoot my shot with Wilder last night, but I knew that was stupid. I had nothing to offer a woman who was searching for true love.

Getting my head on straight had to be my priority. I needed to focus on baseball and be a badass terror on the mound while somehow getting back into the good graces of my teammates.

I couldn't afford to get distracted by some woman, no matter how hot she was.

I had to get to work.

8

———————

CAM

The universe is out to get me. That's all there is to it.

Two weeks had passed since the damned wedding, and I was still obsessing over Wilder. My main focus needed to be baseball, dammit. I'd had a few mediocre outings on the mound, but that was hardly enough to make my mark. I'd never get to New York if I didn't start lighting the baseball world on fire with my pitching. I didn't know what the hell was wrong with me. I was like a stupid, dreamy-eyed teenager drooling over a movie poster of some heartthrob. I kept thinking the feeling would pass, but it hadn't.

And now I was downright pissed off about it.

If I'd been one of those morons who believed in fate, I would swear the universe was trying to tell me something. I never realized how many goddamned songs there were with the word "wild" in them, but I'd heard them all in the last couple of weeks. Every time I turned on the radio I heard stupid shit like "Wildest Dreams" by *The Moody Blues,* a song I hadn't heard in years. Then there was "Wildfire," some song about a horse that my mom used to listen to. And then, just when I thought I was safe, they played "Wild Thing" at the ballpark. I guess it made sense, given the song's connection to the movie *Major League*, but still. It was annoying. Then, when I was riding home from the game on my Harley, I heard "FourFiveSeconds," that Rhianna song about "Wildin."

Every time I heard the name Wilder or something that even came close to it, I had the same odd jolt of adrenaline.

Seriously, what … the fuck … was wrong with me?

I felt like punching something.

The only answer was to go out with her and get her out of my system. It was unlike me to be so obsessed with a woman, and it wasn't as if I knew her at all. Maybe she'd wind up being a raging bitch.

I felt guilty. Though it was true I didn't know her, she seemed very sweet at the wedding. She took good care of her friend, the bride, even though it was tough because she was single at the moment.

Well, she was single as of two weeks ago. For all I knew, she could have found her Prince Charming since then and I'd be left with nothing but my regrets.

There was no time to lose.

Rusty was my only real connection to Wilder, so I figured I would go talk to him.

I texted him to see when he would be working at his bar next, and he told me he'd be there on Wednesday night. That was perfect because it was a rare night off for the Bay Birds.

And since there was no game on and Power Bar and Grill didn't have any special events happening, it was a good time to talk to Rusty.

Before I knew it, Rusty was grinning at me as I slid into the same bar stool I'd sat on last time. Knowing the owner made me feel like a regular, even though I had no intention of staying in Baltimore any longer than I absolutely had to. Still, it was nice to have a place to hang out while I was trapped here. The bar had a comfortable, homey feel to it, with its scent of fried food and fresh beer and smattering of regulars hanging out. Even the music playing in the background was kinda nice, a mix of old and new stuff. At least I was enjoying the music until "Wild World" by Cat Stevens came on.

Sonofabitch.

Maybe it *was* a sign. Who knew?

"What's your pleasure?" he asked.

"Whatever ya got that's good on draft works for me."

Rusty nodded and poured me a mug of an IPA beer he currently had on tap.

"So, what's new with you?" he asked.

I had to tread carefully. If this guy had any clue how I'd been obsessing over Wilder, he'd bust my balls hard. And he'd be right to do it. Figured I'd best ease into it.

"Not much. Pitch, practice, repeat. You know the drill. How was the honeymoon?"

He grinned. Between his slightly sunburned skin and cocky expression, it was clear he'd had a great time. He'd obviously gotten laid a *lot* over the last couple of weeks, and I was jealous. Wasn't like I *couldn't* have gotten some action lately, I just couldn't get Wilder out of my head. Once I got her out of my system, assuming she would give an anti-Prince-Charming like me a second glance, maybe then I could get back to business as usual.

"It was great, man. Really, really great."

He went on to tell me all about the resort where they'd stayed in Hawaii, and I listened as politely as I could. Well, I kinda listened. Not like there was gonna be a test on his trip later. Mostly, I just nodded and waited for him to wrap it up so we could get down to the business at hand.

I sipped my beer and tried to look as casual as possible. "So, I got a question for ya."

"Is that so?" Rusty asked, wiping down the bar and looking like a bartender on TV. I wondered if it really needed cleaning or if he just liked playing the part.

"Yeah. What's the story with Amanda's maid of honor?"

Rusty sighed heavily, which was not what I expected.

"What?" I asked.

"Wilder's a sweet girl, ya know? A really sweet girl," he said.

So much for her being a raging bitch.

"Okayyyy. She still single?"

After hesitating a moment, Rusty said, "Yeah."

"I was thinking of asking her out."

"I see," Rusty said. He clearly wasn't happy.

"What, you think I'm not good enough for her?"

He hesitated; it was all the answer I needed.

"Dude," I said in annoyance, even though he had a point. Rusty still thought of me as the womanizer he'd once roomed with all those years ago. And if I was honest with myself, very little had changed since then.

"I know, I know. I guess I could set you up, but ..."

"But what already?"

"Wilder's a nice girl, you know?"

"And you don't want me to fuck with her."

"Exactly. I mean, she's my wife's best friend." Then Rusty grinned.

"What? What is that smirk?" I asked.

"My wife. I just like the sound of that."

"You are such a pussy."

Rusty shrugged. "Maybe so. And I'm okay with it. I never could have gotten through everything without Amanda."

"Well, yeah. You'd be dead."

He chuckled. "There's that. But it's been pretty tough, not being able to play baseball. She helped me get through all that, and believe me, I was not easy to deal with. I suddenly had to figure out what the hell to do with the rest of my life, and Amanda stayed right by me the whole time. I'm really lucky to have her."

Rusty's words were simple, but I could tell by the intense emotion in his voice and the soft look in his eyes that this man was truly, deeply in love. I couldn't even begin to comprehend that kind of love. Other than Rusty and Amanda, I'd never seen it. Certainly not between my parents.

My feelings for Wilder were nothing more than simple lust. I was sure of it. Pretty sure. But if I didn't confess to having at least some genuine feelings for the woman, Rusty would never give me the go-ahead. Not that I needed his permission, but I had no intention of betraying an old friend. Besides, I had enough enemies in Baltimore already.

Gathering my nerve, I said, "Rusty, I'm not just after a one-night stand here."

Rusty narrowed his eyes at me as if scanning my face for the truth.

"I'm serious," I added.

"Then what are you after?" he asked.

He's gonna make me say it.

"I just ... want to get to know her better. I've been thinking about her a lot since the wedding. Wilder seems really cool and nice, and she's obviously very talented."

Rusty grinned at me.

Here it comes...

"Have a little crush, do we? Are you doodling Mrs. Wilder Becker in your official Bay Birds play book?"

"Not exactly," I said, feeling my face get hot.

He stared at me, those damned blue eyes piercing my soul. "You've really got a thing for her, don't you?"

I sighed heavily, hoping that would be enough of a response for him.

"Wellll?" Rusty asked, taunting me further. I couldn't even get mad. I'd have done the same thing to him, and he damn well knew it.

"Yes, okay? Yes, I guess I have a stupid crush on your beautiful wife's best friend."

Rusty smiled. I knew complimenting Amanda was the way to get to him.

"So ya gonna give me her number or what?" I said, already losing patience. Naturally, that just made Rusty drag the process out even more.

Just like I would have done to him if the situation was reversed.

Stupid karma.

Polishing a glass that likely did not need to be polished, he said, "Well now, I'm not sure I'm at liberty to divulge that information."

I sighed again, which just made Rusty cackle with glee.

"What's your price already?"

"Surely, you're not attempting to *bribe* me?" Rusty said with an annoying twinkle in his eye.

"Yes. I am. What's it gonna take for you to gimme her number?"

"You don't really need my help, do you?" he asked, continuing to tease me. I fought the urge to jump out of my seat and strangle him. But then I reasoned attempted murder might not get me Wilder's contact info any faster.

"Yes," I said through clenched teeth.

"No you don't," Rusty said in a singsong voice. "I'm sure you could find Wilder if you tried. After all, she could be anywhere."

Attempted murder appealed to me more by the second.

Rusty grinned at my furious expression. "She could be *anywhere*," he repeated, then lifted his head to look behind me.

No way.

I turned around, expecting to see Wilder standing right behind me. There was nobody there. Just as I was finalizing my plans to strangle my so-called friend, I spotted her.

She sat at a table facing the window, alone, her back to us. I recognized her long golden-blond hair. I actually gasped, taken aback by the strongest bolt of adrenaline I'd had since last night when I'd damn near been struck in the head by a comebacker baseball from the batter.

Rusty chuckled at my reaction, embarrassing me. I didn't embarrass easily, but I hated feeling vulnerable.

Not wanting to be caught staring at Wilder, I turned back to Rusty.

His expression grew serious.

"Wilder comes here a lot and always sits right there. Know why?"

I shook my head.

"She likes to chill out and relax with a drink, usually while studying lines for a show or an audition. Always faces the window to keep guys from hitting on her. It's the only way to get people to leave her alone."

"Oh."

"She gets hit on a *lot*. So you better bring your A game."

Meeting his gaze, I said, "I will."

Rusty nodded, and I was touched that he was essentially giving his blessing to go after Wilder.

"But dude ... be cool, ya know?" I saw both worry and sadness in Rusty's eyes.

"I will. I swear. I won't do anything to hurt her. I told ya, I'm not looking for a one-night stand."

Though I wasn't sure what I *was* looking for with Wilder, I really wasn't going to try to bag her tonight. I'd had sex with lots of girls on the first date, but not this time. She might not be as emotionally raw as she had been at the wedding, but sleeping with her too fast would be disastrous.

I was getting ahead of myself. The first step was convincing her to let me sit with her at the table. I was rarely nervous before approaching a woman, but this time felt different. Normally when I tried to pick up a woman in a bar, I relied on three things. My good looks, my money, and my celebrity. Something told me none of those things would be all that impressive to Wilder, so I wasn't sure what I was going to say to her. I'd figure out something, I supposed.

I got up from my stool.

"Good luck," Rusty said. The lightness in his tone was back, possibly because he expected me to fail.

Here goes nothing.

I began the long walk over to the table by the window.

9

WILDER

"Excuse me, is this seat taken?" asked a deep voice from a guy hovering over the table where I sat.

I stifled a sigh.

I was really, really not in the mood to be hit on right now. Normally, facing the window did the trick and nobody paid much attention to me.

"No, it's not. You can go ahead and take the chair," I said without looking up.

"Actually, I was wondering if you'd mind if I sat with you."

Damn.

It was worth a shot. Some guys took the hint—and the chair—and went away.

Yes, I minded. I minded very much. The problem was that I just didn't have the emotional stamina to summon up a polite way to say buzz off. Sometimes it was just easier to have a quick chat and then make a hasty exit.

But dammit, I didn't *want* to exit right now. I was having fun all by myself.

After an uncomfortably long pause, I said, "Sure. Go ahead."

I took a few seconds to put on my best actress face so I wouldn't look as annoyed as I felt.

When I finally glanced up at the rando guy, I realized I recognized him.

Camden Becker. He was a pitcher for the Baltimore Bay Birds. I'd always been a casual follower of baseball, but since Amanda was now married to a former player, I took even more of an interest in the team.

"I'm Camden Becker. Or Cam for short."

I waited for him to brag about being a professional baseball player, but he didn't. Interesting.

"Hi, Cam. I'm Wilder Price."

"I know," he said. He seemed nervous. That was unusual, since most guys who hit on me were fairly cocky. I felt a little uncomfortable that he already knew who I was, and he seemed to notice. "I'm a friend of Rusty's."

"Oh, I see."

I turned around to look at Rusty behind the bar. He shrugged. And then he smirked.

Cam couldn't be all bad if he was a friend of Rusty's. And Rusty never would have let Cam approach me if he was a creep.

When I turned back, Cam looked me in the eyes. Such a simple thing, but it was a huge deal to me. I couldn't remember the last time a guy looked me in the eyes instead of at my chest.

He had intense brown eyes, and he was quite handsome. Perhaps it was the intensity itself that I found alluring. I was surprised at the flicker of attraction I felt.

"So, what are you working on?" Cam asked, glancing down at the pages spread out on the table in front of me.

Something in the way he asked the question gave me the impression he was genuinely interested in the answer.

"I'm preparing for an audition," I said, expecting him to get bored immediately. He didn't. Instead, he held his gaze on me, waiting for me to elaborate. "It's for a traveling show of *Beauty and the Beast*."

"Wow. That sounds like it's kind of a big deal."

I smiled. "Yeah. If I get the part it would be incredible."

"You'll get it," Cam said with confidence.

Laughing, I asked, "How can you be so sure?"

"You're an amazing singer, Wilder."

"What?"

Cam cleared his throat. "I, uh ... heard you sing at the wedding."

"Oh, right," I said with a nod. As a friend of Rusty's, naturally he would have been at the wedding. A thrill of excitement went through me knowing this super cute guy had heard me sing. Having guys stare at me because of my looks usually just made me feel cheap, but I'd had a lifelong fantasy about a guy falling for me after hearing me sing. I grew up on Disney films after all.

"That song you sang," Cam continued, looking lost in thought. "It was beautiful."

Either this guy was a terrific actor, or he was genuinely touched by my performance.

I sighed softly, allowing myself to dip even further into my Disney princess fantasy. Was it possible Cam was actually interested in me as a person?

"I'm not exactly the biggest fan of showtunes, but I really enjoyed hearing you sing."

It didn't bother me in the slightest that he didn't like showtunes. Instead, I was thrilled with his honesty. Most guys, if they even bothered to ask about my likes and dislikes, would feign interest in the things I was into. I hated it because I could see through them right away.

"Thank you," I said quietly. Cam's words meant so much to me. Performing was the heart and soul of me, and complimenting my singing was about the nicest thing anyone could do. The best part was, I got the feeling he really meant what he said. This entire conversation felt different than any talk I'd ever had with a man, including my ex-fiancé. It was strange. And wonderful. Even though he was saying all the right things, I didn't get the sense that he was just trying to coax me into bed.

"Have you always been into musicals and stuff?" Cam asked before draining the rest of his beer.

"Yes. Always," I said with a smile. "Ever since I was a little girl, I've always loved the classic Disney movies. Those were my first introduction to musical theater. Then my parents took me to a local production of *Into the Woods* and I was just ... entranced. I'd never seen a live production before, and I was just blown away by the music and the beauty and the power of it. I walked around in a daze afterward. It wasn't long after that when I realized that's what I wanted ... what I *needed* to do for the rest of my life. I'd always loved singing around the house and all, just for fun. I guess I never realized it was something you could do for a living. Not until I saw that show. After that, I was hooked."

I was suddenly self-conscious, talking about such personal stuff to a relative stranger. But one look into Cam's eyes and I knew I hadn't made a mistake.

He was listening. Like, really *listening* to what I was saying.

"Sorry," I said with a soft laugh. "I didn't mean to ramble on like that."

Cam smiled, and my flicker of attraction quickly turned

into a stronger flame of desire. "I like hearing you talk about something you're so passionate about."

Where has this guy been all my life?

I felt bad for talking so much about myself, but it felt so good to be able to express my feelings. Until now, Amanda had been the only one who listened and cared when I talked about stuff like this.

Gesturing to the pages in front of me, I said, "I really hope I get this part. Not only would it be a professional singing job where I could tour all over the country, it just happens to be my dream role."

"Yeah?" he asked with interest.

I nodded. "I know it sounds dumb, but I kinda always identified with Belle."

"Because she's the 'Beauty' to the guy's 'Beast'?" Cam teased.

"N—no. I didn't mean it like that," I stammered.

Cam laughed, a deep and sexy sound. "I'm just kiddin' with ya," he said in his strong New York accent. "Tell me why you feel like Belle."

"Honestly?" I asked, nervous about how real I was gonna get here.

"Yeah. Tell me the honest truth."

"Both because she was an outsider in her town and people thought she was weird, and because men only liked her for her beauty," I said, looking down.

After a moment, Cam said quietly, "That makes sense."

I met his gaze. "Really? You think so?"

"Sure. I can understand why, you know, Belle would get upset if men only wanted her because she was pretty."

Cam sounded so sincere it nearly made me cry.

"But why do you feel like an outsider?"

"Mostly because of my family. Don't get me wrong.

They're not terrible or abusive or anything. It's just ... they don't understand me at all. Believe me, they regret ever taking me to see *Into the Woods*."

"You really think so?" he asked, sounding surprised.

"I know they do. They've said so. My parents are both attorneys, and my sister works in IT. Even though they could easily afford it, my mom and dad refused to pay for my college unless I majored in something 'realistic.' So I had to work to put myself through school to get my theater degree."

"So your parents wanted you to be an accountant or something, and instead you wanted to be a Disney princess." He said it so bluntly that it made me laugh.

"Yes. Exactly."

With a twinkle in his eye, Cam said, "Good for you."

I enjoyed the way he teased me without mocking me or making me feel bad. Like he respected me and my choices. Certainly more than my parents ever did.

"Would you like another drink?" Cam asked.

"Sure. That would be great."

"Coming right up." He stood up and grabbed my empty glass.

I turned to watch him approach the bar. He said something to Rusty, who grinned and fist-bumped him. It was adorable. Cam soon returned to the table with two more beers.

"Thanks," I said, gratefully accepting the drink.

"You're welcome." He sipped his beer. "I really think you got this audition in the bag. You sounded great on the *Little Mermaid* song you did."

Staring at him, I asked, "How did you know I did that song?"

His cheeks reddened, and suddenly his tough New

Yorker image disappeared. "Uh ... well ... uh ... Okay, fine. I looked up your videos online."

"Oh," I said with a laugh. If any other guy had told me he'd stalked my online presence, I probably would have been creeped out by it. With Cam, it was endearing. "That's very sweet."

"I just ... you know ... like I told ya, I liked hearing you sing at the wedding, and I wanted to hear some more." He averted his gaze, focusing on his beer instead of me. I stifled a dreamy sigh. Could this guy be any cuter?

Still, I hated that he was so uncomfortable. I could tell he was not a man who liked being vulnerable. I needed to change the subject, and quickly.

"You had quite an outing last night," I said.

Cam seemed confused.

"On the mound," I added.

His eyes lit up. "You're a baseball fan? You know who I am?"

"Yes, and yes. I'm not as big a fan as Amanda, but I've followed the Bay Birds since I was a kid."

"Nice," he said with a smile.

As I gazed into his eyes, I felt a deep connection with him. I could tell by his expression—the familiar look of longing tinged with a hint of despair—that he felt the same way about playing baseball as I did about performing. In that moment, I knew I was in the presence of a truly kindred spirit.

"Do you like playing for the Bay Birds?" I asked, eager to give him a chance to talk about his dreams.

After a moment of hesitation, he said, "No."

"*Really?*"

"They're okay, I guess. Just not the team I want to play for," Cam said, his brown eyes full of sadness.

"Who do you want to play for?"

"The New York Kings."

"Oh, that makes sense."

He raised an eyebrow in surprise.

"You tawk like yawah from Noo Yawak," I said.

He laughed that deep laugh of his, sending a tingle through my body.

"That's pretty impressive," he said with a sexy grin.

I shrugged. "Sometimes I have to do accents when I'm in a show."

"Well, you're very good at it."

"Thanks. I'm sorry you're not happy here in Baltimore," I told him.

"I figure I'm not here forever. I guess I can stand it for a while. But let me ask you something. *What* is the *deal* with people here putting the Maryland flag on everything?"

I laughed, allowing myself to imagine he found my laugh sexy as well. Probably not, but it was fun to pretend.

"I know. We love our flag in this state," I said, glancing around at the decor on the walls of Power Bar and Grill. I counted at least three versions of the flag, including a wooden sign, a baseball bat with the flag image, and a decorative flag dinner plate.

Giggling, I pulled out my wallet and held it up to him. It, too, sported the familiar black, yellow, red, and white Maryland flag.

"*Damn*, you people are obsessed with that thing," Cam said, shaking his head and chuckling.

"Yup," I said proudly.

"I guess Baltimore has its ... charms." He wrinkled his nose. "It's just not where I want to be."

"I get that," I said. "If it makes you feel any better, I'd rather be in New York too."

"Really?" Cam sounded excited by the idea. "Oh, well yeah, that makes sense. Broadway."

"Exactly," I said with a smile.

"I feel bad. It's not like it's a secret that I'm not thrilled to be here. Pretty sure the guys on the team all hate me," he said, toying with a paper napkin on the table.

"Oh, that's right," I blurted out without thinking.

"What?"

"Sorry. I just remembered talking to Amanda about you when you first came to town."

"Is that so?" Cam asked with a smirk.

"Yeah," I said, deciding to just dig in further. Something told me it was okay to be totally upfront with him. "You had lots to say about the city when you first got here, didn't you? She and I were like 'What is this guy's problem'?"

Cam chuckled. "That's fair. Not my finest moment."

"You called the city Bodymore, Murderland."

"Uh, yeah. I did," he admitted.

"Really, Mistah Noo Yawak? You gonna tawak about our murdah rate?"

Cam laughed again, and the sound was so hot, I wanted to grab him by the collar and kiss him right there.

He held his hands up in mock defense, "Okay, okay. Again, a fair point." He sighed. "Honestly, I do feel kinda bad about that. I want to be in New York and not here, but that's not the team's fault. I shouldn't have talked shit about the city. I don't blame the guys for hating me."

My heart went out to him. He just seemed so sad.

"I'm sure they'll warm up to you. Give it time."

Cam shrugged.

"I guess New York was your team when you were growing up?"

"Yeah."

His response was so simple, but the deep fondness in his eyes said more than his words. And something in the way he looked at me told me he knew I understood. And I did. I really did. I understood what it meant to want something so much it hurt.

"I hope you get there someday. Maybe the best way to work toward that is to get really good while you're here."

His eyes flashed with determination. "Yeah. Believe me, that's what I'm gonna do. Show New York what I got and show Atlanta what they gave away."

I'd forgotten that I'd read he had been let go by the Atlanta Suns. My heart hurt for him, as I saw the pain in his eyes. Again, it was a pain I knew all too well. The life of a performer was filled with rejection. Some days it felt like that was all there was to it.

"And not just for my sake," he continued. "It's the right thing for the Bay Birds. Whether I want to be here or not, they're my team right now and I owe them my very best." He sighed deeply.

"What?"

"I really do feel bad about some of the stuff I said. About Baltimore and ... other stuff."

"What other stuff?"

"Kinda talked shit about Brady Keaton."

"Really? Brady?" I asked, unable to hide my shock.

"I know, I know," Cam said, fiddling with his napkin. "Hometown hero. All around nice guy."

"He is." I remembered Amanda telling me how Brady had comforted her on the field the day she saved Rusty's life. Brady was a great guy. Loved Baltimore with all his heart, and the quickest way to anger him was to talk smack about his hometown.

"I know I should apologize. I'm not great with that kind of thing."

I nodded, not surprised to hear that. Cam seemed nice enough, but he had an intense gruffness about him. As much as I hated to admit it, I was kind of turned on by it.

Something caught Cam's attention behind me, and he nodded.

"I think Rusty's ready to close for the night." He sounded disappointed.

"How long have we been talking?" I asked, surprised at how late it was.

"Quite a while, apparently," Cam said in a deep, husky voice, staring into my eyes.

My breath caught in my throat. Being with Cam was positively *addictive*. I couldn't remember the last time anyone made me feel like this.

Probably because it had never happened before.

I didn't care how late it was. I wasn't ready for this magical evening to end.

"Do you wanna go back to my place?" he asked.

Earlier this evening I would never have dreamed of letting a guy take me home from the bar. Now I was struggling to come up with a reason to say no. I'd only had a few one-night stands in my life, and they'd all been depressing disasters. I'd never *not* regretted having one. But everything about my encounter with Cam tonight seemed so different.

"Wait," he said, and I feared he was about to retract his offer. "Wilder, you should know ... I'm not looking for anything serious right now."

I had to dig deep in my bag of acting tricks to hide my gut reaction to that statement.

"I'm not the type to settle down, you know?"

I nodded, still making a strong effort to hide my disappointment.

"Okay," I said softly.

"I wanted to be upfront with you is all," he said. The napkin was now completely shredded in his hands.

"I appreciate that. I'd love to go back to your place."

Cam's eyes flew open wide. He hadn't expected that.

I hadn't either. I hadn't known what my answer would be until the words came out of my mouth. All I knew was I couldn't bear having this amazing night come to an end. Not yet.

"But ... I'm not making any promises, okay? Can we just continue our discussion at your place?"

The gentleness in his expression floored me.

"Sure. Let's go."

10

WILDER

I followed Cam in my own car to his place. Staring at him looking sexy as hell on his Harley motorcycle, I was grateful to have a few minutes alone to get my head on straight. After my last one-night stand, I'd promised myself I would never do it again. The entire experience had been so awful. Depressing and degrading. Once we got down to business, it became clear pretty quickly that he had no intention of satisfying my needs. The whole thing was over fast, which was probably for the best. It was like having sex with an inexperienced, horny teenager. A lot of frantic humping on his part and then it was over.

Afterward, he couldn't remember my name.

It was a stupid idea. I never should have done it. Yet another dirty little secret that nobody seemed to know. Pretty girls get lonely too.

I'd had other women tell me with jealousy in their voices that it must be nice to be able to take home any guy you want at any time. The reality of the situation was so much uglier than people thought. Yes, I could probably have my pick of hot guys, but it wasn't necessarily a good thing.

That sexy guy with the chiseled face and bulging muscles who wouldn't give a plain girl a second glance? He was usually no prize once you got him home.

After that experience with—well, to be fair, I'd forgotten his name now too—I swore to myself I'd never have another one-night stand as long as I lived. That was one of the reasons I'd been so guarded at Amanda's wedding. I'd felt awfully vulnerable, so I took care with how much I drank and who I talked to.

I stared at the taillights of Cam's bike in front of me at a stoplight, realizing I was damned lucky I hadn't met him at the reception. He was hard enough to resist now, let alone in my lonely bridesmaid state of mind.

As we both turned into the parking garage at Cam's apartment building, I kept waiting for the panic and regret to set in. So far, it hadn't. I didn't intend to sleep with him tonight, but going back to a man's apartment on the first date was kind of a big deal.

And he'd said he wasn't looking for a serious relationship.

It figures.

As much as I'd hated to hear those words out of Cam's mouth, I deeply appreciated his honesty. I respected how firm he was when he spoke, making sure I knew the score. And I'd been just as forthright with him, not wanting to be a tease and let him think he was definitely getting laid.

Honestly, I wasn't sure what would happen tonight.

By the time I parked my car and got out, Cam was already standing close by in the garage. A small ripple of apprehension went through me as I worried about what I had gotten myself into. And yet when I caught Cam's gaze, something in his eyes told me everything would be okay. He didn't smile, but that didn't bother me. The intensity in his face reminded me of why I'd come here in the first place. To continue our wonderful conversation.

Cam led me through the fancy lobby and up to his apartment. His place was on the small side, but a luxury apartment, nonetheless. I headed straight over to the huge bank of windows overlooking the city.

"Wow, this is an incredible view," I said, drinking in the twinkling lights of the city below.

"Yeah, it's okay I guess," Cam said with a shrug as he walked over to join me.

"Okay because it's 'just Baltimore,'" I said with a grin.

"Exactly," he said gruffly, making me giggle. Cam seemed surprised by my response, but it was refreshing to have a man be so truthful with me. He wasn't gonna pretend to be a huge fan of musicals or that he liked the city of Baltimore just because he knew I cared about those things. He wasn't mean about it, but he wasn't bullshitting me, either.

"The city will grow on you, Cam. You'll see."

"Don't hold your breath," he said, shooting the streets below an annoyed glance.

Cam stood next to me patiently while I gazed out the window for a little while longer. I enjoyed the fact that he didn't rush me. He didn't even speak until I turned away from the window to face him.

"Would you like a drink?" he asked.

"No, I better not. I'll have to drive home later," I said, both because I wanted to be responsible and to remind him that I wasn't going to spend the night here.

He nodded and walked to the kitchen to pour himself a drink.

I headed over to the big, fluffy brown couch in the living room and sat. Drink in hand, Cam joined me. He sat a comfortable distance away from me as if he genuinely planned to continue our talk rather than get physical right away.

Gesturing at his glass, I said, "There's something really sexy about a guy who drinks whiskey."

That earned me one of those slight, corner of the mouth grins men do. I found that even sexier than his drink.

Laying back on the couch, I said, "This is so comfortable."

I wasn't only talking about the furniture, either. Everything about this evening felt good.

"It's okay, I guess. Just had to grab whatever was available on short notice," he said with a grimace. Though I was pretty sure he didn't want to talk about it, I could tell his being traded so suddenly had been very painful for him.

I wanted to say something to get his mind off his troubles, but I didn't know him well enough to know what to say. Cam was quiet now, lost in his thoughts. And they didn't seem like happy thoughts to me.

"Your Harley is beautiful," I said, taking a stab at lighter conversation.

Cam rewarded me instantly with another smile, making my lady parts tingle dangerously.

"Thanks," was all he said, but I'd felt his mood lift instantly.

"Bet you and Trace Ridgerton have a lot to talk about," I added, making him chuckle deep in his throat.

"Hell yeah," Cam said. "That dude has strong opinions on why he thinks Indian bikes are better than Harleys. He's outta his damn mind."

"You like having him catch for you?"

"I do," he said. "I got real lucky in that department, I'll say that for the Bay Birds. Trace can catch a good game. Even helped me perfect my changeup pitch. And my slurve.

Keeps saying he thinks I can master a two-seamer fastball, but I'm not sure about that."

I smiled. I should have realized talking baseball was the way to get him to really open up.

"That's great. You do seem to make a great team."

"Yeah," he said, but didn't elaborate. So much for getting him to open up. Still, I could see his mind whirring, even if his mouth was fairly quiet. For the moment, I'd gotten him thinking about his current baseball situation and not the one he'd recently had to leave behind.

Since Cam obviously wasn't about to pour his heart out to me right now, I couldn't help but steer the conversation back to my interests.

"I love that you found my singing videos online, Cam," I said gently.

His body stiffened, and I could tell he was still a little embarrassed about having accidentally admitted that.

"Did you have a favorite song?"

Cam shrugged. "Not really."

His response disappointed me a little and he seemed to pick up on it.

"I told ya, I don't know much about showtunes, and I definitely don't know much about Disney," he said, making a face.

Cam's grimace at the word "Disney" made me giggle. Odd that I would find his disgust at something I adored so funny, but I did.

"I only know the more famous musicals. You know, like stuff from *Les Miz* and shit. You have such a pretty voice, Wilder. I mean, you'd have to if you were able to—"

"To what?"

Cam seemed uncomfortable. "To keep me watching those videos for so long."

"Like how long?"

He chuckled, finally seeming to relax a bit. "Couple hours."

I laughed, and his shoulders relaxed even more.

"Showtunes are just ... well, they just *really* aren't my thing, but somehow it was different when it was you singing."

"Wow," I said softly. "High praise indeed."

He stared at me, those brown eyes suddenly looking quite serious.

"What?"

Hesitating a moment before he spoke, Cam said, "That one was really pretty. The one from *Les Miz*. I mean, they were all really great, but that one ... yeah."

Coming from him, it was a huge compliment.

"Thank you," I said, my voice practically a whisper.

Cam set down his glass on the coffee table. My breath caught in my lungs as I waited to see what he would do next.

He stared at me with those deep, soulful eyes. I stared back, still breathless. He seemed to be feeling me out, trying to figure out whether or not I'd allow him to kiss me.

I didn't move a muscle, not wanting to give him any reason not to go for it.

Cam made his move, drawing close to where I still lay back against the couch. He cupped my face in a way I'd only seen men do in the movies and pressed his lips to mine.

Wrapping my arms around his neck, I eagerly returned his kiss, breathing in his scent of pure masculinity. That delicious combination of whiskey and expensive cologne that was uniquely Cam Becker.

Every part of my body seemed to instinctively respond to this man. My lips were on fire, my nipples tingled, and my panties were wet.

In that instant, with that one kiss, I knew without a shred of doubt that I wanted to have sex with this man right then and there. I didn't care if it was stupid. I didn't care that I would likely regret it tomorrow. And I didn't care about my vow to never, ever take another guy home from a bar and sleep with him.

All I cared about was getting Cam Becker inside of me as soon as humanly possible.

I grabbed his right hand and moved it down to my breast, wanting him to know exactly what I was thinking. Right now, I didn't want nuance or subtleness.

I wanted *him.*

Cam got the message. I could tell from the deep animal growl in his throat. Before I even knew what was happening, we were on the floor. I hadn't even noticed that he had pushed the coffee table out of the way. All I could concentrate on was *him.* His huge hands, his hard, muscled chest, and his manly scent that drove me out of my mind.

His hands pinned me down and he had a wild look in his eye that was both scary and sexy.

Cam's breath was heavy when he managed to say, "Are you sure about this? This is awfully ... fast."

I let out a deep, dreamy sigh. Even in the heat of the moment, he still made sure this was what I wanted. Most of the guys I'd been with would have already orgasmed by now. None of them worried that things were happening too fast.

"Yes," I said, already unbuttoning his shirt.

Cam grabbed my hands. At first, his roughness startled me. Then I realized what he was doing.

"Wilder," he said, his eyes boring into mine. "Are. You. Sure."

His question sounded more like a statement. A deadly serious one.

I managed to pull my hands out of his grasp and gently caressed his cheek. "Yes, I'm sure. I want this. I want you. *Now.*"

He nodded, and there was an instant change in his demeanor. His hesitation and concern were replaced by that Cam Becker intensity which had riled me up in the first place. I was ready to explode. If, like most guys, he didn't bother to get me off, I'd have to set my vibrator to the highest level when I got home tonight.

I'd never been so aroused in my life. It was practically painful.

Once I'd torn off his shirt, I tried to unbutton his pants. It was taking too long, for both of us, so he jumped up and stripped for me.

Then he stripped me of my clothes.

When I was completely naked, Cam took time to admire my body.

In that moment, it occurred to me that we'd spent the entire night talking and he'd never once mentioned my physical appearance. Because of that, and the way he looked at me now with the fire of desire in his eyes, he made me feel like he was attracted to *me*. As a person. As a woman. For the first time in my life, I didn't just feel pretty. I felt *desirable.*

Cam bent down to kiss me, bringing his delightful scent close to me again. His kisses grew more passionate, more desperate, and I ached for him to ram inside me.

"I need," he panted, "to go get protection."

"IUD," was all I said.

"Thank God," he said, not missing a beat.

He was making me crazy. I wanted to scream at him to fuck me and do it *now.*

I never used the word "fuck" when it came to sex, but Cam seemed to bring out that side of me.

Even in his desperation, maddeningly, he took his time. He kissed down my neck, and then began licking my nipples.

I moaned out loud. After so many years of bad sex, I'd forgotten about foreplay. Most guys would be on their way home by now.

Cam's kisses traveled farther and farther down my body. Before I knew it, he was spreading my legs.

Then I felt his tongue brush my most sensitive spot. Bucking my hips, I cried out.

Foreplay wasn't the only thing guys rarely did for me.

As his tongue swirled around and around my clit, I closed my eyes, moaning with sheer ecstasy. Somehow Cam immediately found the perfect rhythm to drive me completely out of my mind.

I lay on the floor, legs spread, while the sexiest man I'd ever met in my life pleasured me beyond my wildest sexual desires. I could hardly believe this was real. That it was actually happening.

My orgasm began to build, the first one given to me by a man in God knows how long. I hoped the walls weren't too thin, because I started screaming and didn't know how to stop.

I screamed Cam's name and God's name and who knew what else as my body rocked and spasmed. I came harder and harder, as wave after wave of ecstasy slammed into me until my body went slack.

Cam made his way back up to where I lay panting on the floor.

"How was that?" he murmured in my ear.

I responded with a low, satisfied moan.

He chuckled deep in his throat. "Mission accomplished then," he said, then kissed my neck like he had just before giving me the best orgasm of my life. "I need to be inside you."

"I need that too," I said, closing my eyes and reveling in his touch. I admired his restraint in thoroughly satisfying me first, but it was definitely his turn.

Cam pinned my hands down once again. I loved how *powerful* he was when he was on top of me. He seemed so in control, even though he must be desperate by now.

I cried out when he slid into me at last. Again, I closed my eyes so I could enjoy the delicious, erotic sensation of Cam sliding in and out of my body, still tingling from my earth-shattering climax. Deeply sensual growls emanated from his throat, adding to the excitement of pure animal sex.

When I opened my eyes, Cam was focused on my face as he pumped himself in and out of me. A sharp bolt of renewed attraction and adrenaline went through me when our eyes met. I felt a deep connection with him that I'd never felt with anyone else in bed. For once, it didn't feel like he was having sex with just my body. It felt like he was having sex with *me*.

His thrusts became faster and more desperate, and yet it was nothing like any sexual experience I'd had. Cam wasn't some overgrown frat guy just trying to get off while using my body as a vessel. He made me feel like he was desperate not just for orgasmic release, but desperate to be with me.

Gazing deeply into my eyes, Cam said breathlessly, "You're an amazing woman, Wilder."

Simple words but filled with tremendous meaning. He called me an amazing woman. Not beautiful, but *amazing*.

And he also remembered my name.

That it meant so much made me realize how low I'd set the bar before.

"Wilder," he repeated as if reading my mind. He said my name two more times, but now; it came out as more like a groan. He was close.

"Cam," I cried out, throwing my head back to show him how much pleasure he was giving me. For once, no acting was required.

He let out the deepest, most primal growl yet. He'd reached his peak at last. Collapsing on top of me, he murmured my name once more.

He rolled off of me and propped himself up on his elbow. He suddenly looked sad, which was the last thing I'd expected. I wondered what in the world was going through his mind.

"What?" I asked, worried.

"I'm sorry you're on the floor," he said, tenderly stroking my hair. "That wasn't exactly my plan. Just kinda ... happened."

"It's okay," I said. "More than okay. Cam, that was absolutely incredible."

"Well, you're an incredible woman," he said, still running his fingers through my hair.

Incredible. Not beautiful. And he stroked my hair. No man had ever done that.

A ripple of apprehension went through me as I realized I could really fall for this man.

Pretty sure I already had.

"I don't usually do stuff like this," I said. "You know, sex on the first date."

Cam nodded but said nothing. The message was clear.

He couldn't say the same.

It was a splash of cold, hard reality, but I guess it was what I needed. He was not the boyfriend type. It was heartbreaking, but it was still better than if he'd lied or strung me along.

My emotions churning, I sat up. No sense in prolonging the inevitable.

"Well, I'd better get going."

He stood and held out a hand to help me to my feet. I stifled a dreamy sigh.

If Cam hadn't come right out and told me he was not the type to settle down, I might never have known. He seemed so perfect. Well, he seemed perfect for me at least.

We got dressed, then I turned to say goodnight.

Or maybe it was goodbye. I wasn't sure.

"Wilder," he began.

I held my breath. His tone was serious, like he was about to say something important.

"Uh ... drive safe, okay?"

"I will," I said, feeling the tears form in the back of my throat.

I'd thought having meaningless, empty sex with a stranger was the worst feeling in the world.

Turned out having feelings for the guy was way worse.

I managed a smile for Cam as I headed for the door.

11

CAM

The floor.

I fucked Wilder on the *floor*.

I stared at the door for a moment after she left and then staggered over to the couch and flopped down. What in the hell had I been thinking? I remembered all the things she'd said at the wedding about how she was looking for her Prince Charming. She was searching for that forever kind of love.

Instead, she got me tonight.

My eyes landed on the carpet where I'd banged Wilder like she was some cheap prostitute. Goddammit, that was not how tonight was supposed to go. I hadn't intended to have sex with her at all on the first date, never mind like that.

And yet the whole experience had been mind-blowingly awesome. Wilder had certainly seemed to enjoy it. I could still hear her screams of ecstasy when I made her come.

Somehow, being with her felt so natural and utterly different than with any other woman.

I couldn't help grinning slightly when I recalled the way

Wilder looked post-sex, with her blond hair all messed up and the expression of a woman who was good and thoroughly satisfied. Just like I'd fantasized she would look after sex with me.

I got up from the couch and wandered over to the window, remembering how impressed Wilder had been by the view. It was beautiful at night, even if it was Baltimore and not New York. Staring out the window, I thought over the events of this evening. And not just the sex, either. I'd enjoyed talking with Wilder more than I ever had with anyone. Ever. I loved listening to her talk about how much she loved performing. Though I didn't know the first thing about trying to make it as a professional singer, I knew what it meant to throw yourself into your life's passion. I totally got that.

I'd brought her back to my place because I hadn't wanted the evening to end. I really hadn't expected to have sex with her. I'd done my best to be totally honest with her, not making any promises about the future, and telling her upfront I wasn't a serious relationship kind of guy.

And she'd slept with me anyway.

I'd thought having sex with Wilder would finally get her out of my system, but I was sorely mistaken about that. I was more obsessed with her than ever, and I found that rather frightening. Because it wasn't just her body I was lusting after. That, I was used to. That, I could handle. But Wilder brought up a bunch of jumbled up emotions that I had no idea what to do with.

Normally, I would forget about a woman once she left my apartment. And I was fairly sure the woman wouldn't give me a second thought either. That was fine. It worked for both of us. It made sense.

This whole situation with Wilder did not.

Chatting with a woman and actually *enjoying* it was something I was entirely unaccustomed to. Such a simple thing, and yet I could hardly make sense of it because it had never happened before. Until now, talking to a woman at a bar was nothing more than a prelude to sex. Technically, that was what had happened tonight, but for once it hadn't been my plan. All I'd really wanted at the beginning of the evening was to get to know Wilder better. Sex had been an incredible, unexpected bonus.

Enjoying a friendly talk with a woman felt odd to me, because all I'd ever seen my parents do was scream and fight. Not for a moment did they ever seem to enjoy each other. I wasn't exactly sure how my talk with Wilder had gone so well, and I was even less sure about how to make it happen again. I had to be very careful about what I said so I wouldn't screw this up with her. My big, stupid mouth was forever getting me in trouble.

For example, the time I made my parents get divorced.

The writing had been on the wall for a long time, of course. My logical brain knew that my mom and dad had despised each other for years, and that I hadn't caused them to hate each other. Still, there was the fateful day when I was fourteen and had reached the limits of my patience when my mom had narrowly missed hitting my dad in the head with a mug she'd thrown in his direction. I remember yelling, *"If you hate each other so damn much, why don't you just fucking get divorced?"*

And they did.

It doesn't take a psychiatry expert to explain how much that fucked me up as a kid.

Right now, at the top of the list of my jumbled emotions was worry. I worried that Wilder hadn't planned on having sex with me so quickly, and I hoped like hell she didn't regret it. I could tell she was the type of woman who felt things deeply, which meant she could easily get hurt.

I sighed and closed my eyes, remembering why I'd decided to leave her alone at the wedding when she was super vulnerable. Was she feeling that way now?

Staring out at the city again, I wondered if she would tell Amanda we'd slept together. They were best friends, so it was pretty likely. And then Amanda would tell Rusty.

Rusty might be pissed off at me. He'd seemed protective of her, reluctant to set me up with her.

And yet if Wilder was upset, Rusty might know about it.

I still couldn't believe I'd had sex with her like I was some overgrown frat boy. I didn't even hold her afterward. I mean, I never did that, but the women I was usually with never seemed to care. They wanted to get laid just like me. But Wilder was different. She deserved to be gently held and cared for, but I didn't know if I was capable of that.

Drive safe.

That was all I'd said to her.

What the hell was wrong with me?

Staring out into the darkness, I hoped like hell Wilder was okay.

THE NEXT NIGHT's game ran late, and I rushed over to Power Bar and Grill as quickly as I could after thirteen innings were in the books. Good thing I hadn't pitched tonight.

I managed to catch Rusty just as he was locking up.

"Hey, man," I said, out of breath but pretending not to be. I didn't think I fooled him.

"Hey. You all right?" he asked with a quizzical look.

"Yeah. Sure. Fine."

Rusty nodded, clearly unconvinced. "I know it was a long game. Sorry you missed us." He glanced toward the door he had just locked. No doubt he was tired and just wanted to go home to Amanda. But I had to know what, if anything, he knew about Wilder's state of mind.

"Yeah. Thought the game would never end," I said, my mind spinning as I tried to come up with something to keep Rusty here for a few minutes so we could talk.

"What already?" he asked bluntly.

I was relieved he had cut to the chase. "I slept with Wilder last night."

Rusty's blue eyes opened wide. That answered my question about whether Wilder had talked to Amanda yet.

"You did?" he asked. "Wow."

I'd expected him to be mad, but his expression was unreadable.

"I swear, I hadn't planned on it."

"I knew you two left together, but I figured maybe you were just walking her to her car. You know, like a *gentleman*."

And there it was. The hard edge in his voice was unmistakable.

"We went back to my place. Just to talk."

"Uh-huh," he said, slumping against the brick wall outside of his bar.

"Yeah. Okay. I wouldn't believe me either."

Turning his head toward me, Rusty said sharply, "Wilder never does stuff like that you know. Sleep with a guy on the first date. As far as I know, anyway."

"I know, I know. And that's why I wanted to talk to you. To see if you've heard from her. I just wanna make sure she's okay.'

"Why don't you just call her?" he asked.

"Umm ... well ..."

"Well, what?"

"I didn't … I didn't exactly get her number."

"You had sex with her, but you didn't get her phone number."

"Correct."

"Asshole," he grumbled, but with a laugh.

"Also correct."

Rusty chuckled again.

"It all happened so fast. I just kinda forgot. But look, I want you to know I was totally upfront with her. I told her *before* we did anything that I wasn't looking for a serious relationship."

"Really?" he asked, looking confused. "And she still slept with you?"

"Yeah."

"Hmmm." Rusty didn't seem as mad as he had a few seconds ago, but I still worried he might not give me Wilder's number. "What do you think of her?"

I thought about acting tough, pretending I didn't care. After all, that was my default setting.

"She's pretty cool, actually," I admitted quietly.

He grinned at me. "Interesting."

"I like her, okay? Happy now?" I grumbled.

Rusty laughed, sounding quite happy indeed.

"So can I have her number, or would you rather stand out here all night talking to me instead of going home to your beautiful wife?"

That made him smile. Mentioning Amanda worked every time.

He pulled his phone out of his back pocket and sent me a text with Wilder's phone number. I just hoped he'd sent me the real one and wasn't pranking me with some pizza joint's number.

Rusty shook his head at me, making *tsk-tsk* noises.

"I cannot believe you had intimate relations with that woman and you didn't even get her phone number. I bet you don't even know her real name."

Huh?

"Goodnight!" Rusty said brightly before walking off into the night.

12

WILDER

C am was pitching today.

Normally, I kept the game on in the background at home while I did other things, but today I couldn't keep my eyes off the TV. Well, I couldn't keep my eyes off *him*. Cam was so intense when he pitched.

I got chills as I watched him stare down the batter from the mound. I loved when the camera showed a closeup of him as he wound up to pitch. He struck out the first batter he faced, and my heart leapt with excitement. I always wanted to see my Bay Birds win, but I was more invested this time. I was clapping one moment and groaning the next. Watching a simple baseball game was a rollercoaster of emotions now.

Which was worrisome to say the least. Thank goodness Cam had been so upfront about not wanting to be in a relationship, because I definitely would have been expecting something more after our first incredible date. We seemed to have such an amazing connection. I rarely talked to anyone so freely about myself, never mind someone I just met. And with any other man, I would have felt cheap and used after having sex on the floor like that, but I didn't. Not at all. I wasn't sure why, but it was just different with Cam. He didn't treat me like I was nothing more than a one-night stand.

Even if that was what I'd turned out to be.

A tiny yet stupid part of me wondered if it were possible that Cam would ever consider changing his mind about not being a relationship person. But such thoughts were dangerous. He wouldn't likely all of a sudden become boyfriend material just for me.

My thoughts and emotions were all over the place right now. Good thing I had plans to meet up with Amanda later. She was always the perfect sounding board for my messy life.

Staring at Cam looking sexy on the mound, I wondered what I was getting myself into.

AMANDA and I squealed and hugged each other on her doorstep. I'd been so busy at work that I hadn't seen her since she and Rusty got back from their honeymoon. Since I tended bar at a fancy steak restaurant, I was often unavailable on the weekends. We'd agreed to hang out this afternoon at her place so we could catch up.

We headed out to her large, screened-in porch at the back of her house. It was the perfect spot to be on a warm afternoon in June, out of the direct sun but still outside. We settled into a couple of comfy wicker chairs, sitting across from each other so we could talk. The view across the acres of land was breathtaking, and I could smell the fresh cut grass.

Amanda's dogs, Lucky and Renner, followed us out to the porch, but Rusty wasn't home. That worked for me. Her dogs would keep all my secrets.

Renner, the black lab, came over to me, looking for attention. I happily obliged, scritching his cute little head. Lucky was shyer, but he would approach me eventually. He always did.

"Here ya go," Amanda said with a smile as she handed me a glass of wine.

"Thanks." I drew in a deep breath and let it out, feeling more relaxed even before sipping the wine. Being here with my bestie was just what I needed.

"So, tell me all about your honeymoon," I said. "I saw Rusty at the bar, and he clearly got some sun."

"Yes, he sure did," Amanda said. "I kept slathering him with sunscreen, but you know how it is with gingers."

I nodded, sipping my wine. Amanda looked well rested and happy, which made me happy in turn. She showed me pictures on her phone of their fabulous trip to Hawaii. The weather was lovely, but it could have rained every day and she still would have had a great time. She and Rusty always had fun as long as they were together.

"Looks like you had a great time," I said, scrolling through the photos. The two of them looked so happy and in love. I felt like a bad friend because seeing their happiness made me a little sad. Some days it just seemed impossible I would ever find love like that. This was one of those days, I supposed.

I took another sip of wine, hoping it would rekindle my earlier feelings of relaxation. The alcohol certainly didn't hurt.

"So, did you have fabulous honeymoon sex every single day?" I asked.

"Wilderrrr ..."

I smiled. "Your blush tells me that's a yes."

"Maybe not *every* day, but a lot, yeah," she said with a laugh. "It was wonderful. *He* was wonderful."

"That's great. I'm really happy for you."

"Okay, enough about me," she said, putting her phone away. "What about you? What have you been up to lately?"

Whooo boy, that's a loaded question.

Amanda didn't seem to suspect I'd been up to anything unusual, so if Cam had by some chance told Rusty about what had happened between us, he clearly hadn't told her. Not surprising—Rusty was hardly the gossipy type.

"Oh, you know. Working a lot. Still preparing for the *Beauty and the Beast* audition."

She clasped her hands together and squealed. "Ooh, it's coming up soon, isn't it?"

"Yup."

"That's so exciting. I want you to get the part so bad, but I will miss you like crazy while you're traveling all over the country performing," Amanda said, hoisting her wine glass in my direction.

A ripple of excitement went through me just thinking about the possibilities. Playing Belle in the traveling show would be the biggest opportunity of my career. And it was my absolute *dream* part. It meant so much to me, sometimes I was scared to even think about it too much. Mostly, I was focused on preparing for my audition and hoping for the best.

I took a sip of wine. Then I said as casually as I could, "Oh hey, do you know Cam Becker?"

Amanda nodded. "Yeah. I mean, I don't know him well. He and Rusty go way back. They were roommates for a little while before either of them made it to the majors. Why do you ask?"

"I slept with him," I said bluntly.

Amanda jerked her hand in surprise, sloshing her wine in the process. Carefully, she set the wineglass down, staring at me all bug-eyed.

I giggled. I couldn't help it. It was rare to have something exciting to talk about these days, so I'd had no desire to sugarcoat it.

"Wh—what?" Amanda sputtered. "How did you ... When did you ... How do you even know him?" After taking a brief moment to collect herself, she reached over and touched my arm with concern. "Most importantly, are you okay?"

She knew all about my past experiences with men and how awful I usually felt afterwards. The only man I'd really been comfortable with in bed was my ex-fiancé, and that had turned into an utter disaster. After his betrayal, I'd tried having casual sex, both to soothe my bruised ego and find out what I was missing. Turned out I hadn't been missing much. Amanda knew I'd sworn off of one-night stands, so no wonder she was shocked by my statement.

"Yes, I'm okay. At least I think I am," I said. All my mixed emotions about what had happened between Cam and I came bubbling up all over again. "I met him at Power one night. I was sitting at my usual table studying my lines. And he came over to talk to me."

"I'm surprised Rusty didn't run interference for you. Or was he not there that night? Were we still on our honeymoon?"

"No, he was there. This was right after you guys got back. I'm not sure, but I think Cam might have checked with

Rusty before he came over to talk to me," I said with a smile, remembering Rusty's smirk that night.

"Ah, I see," Amanda said. She knew I blew off, or to be fair, I gently let down ninety-nine percent of the guys who hit on me. She knew there had to have been a reason I even spoke to Cam Becker that night, let alone slept with him.

"At first, I didn't want to talk to him. You know how I am when I go to the bar and sit in the back. I just want to chill, have a drink, and study my lines. *Alone.*"

Amanda nodded in understanding.

"But when he said he was a friend of Rusty's, I figured it would be rude to just blow him off." I paused for a moment, lost in the sweet memories of the deep conversation we'd had. "And almost right away, talking with Cam felt different from any other guy."

"Really?" Amanda asked curiously. "How so?"

"Well, for one thing, he didn't brag about being a pitcher for the Bay Birds right away. I knew who he was of course, but I didn't let on. It kinda felt like he was introducing himself to me as a real person and not as a famous athlete."

"I see what you mean. I figure most guys would lead with the *do you know who I am?'* angle if they happen to be famous."

"Exactly! That's the thing about these players. If you're a Bay Birds fan, you know who they are. If not, they'll have to tell you that they're semi-famous, but he didn't. But Amanda, the most incredible thing was, Cam *listened to me* when I talked."

"You're kidding," she said with a laugh. "That's amazing."

"It was amazing," I said quietly. "Nobody listens to me. Not men, anyway."

"I know," she said with a sad smile. Being born pretty

gave me a number of ridiculously unfair advantages in this world, so I really tried not to complain about the drawbacks. And yet it could be very painful when people simply stared at me all the time and didn't really give a damn about me as a person. Since Amanda was my dearest friend, I did vent to her about the issue from time to time, and she seemed to understand. Not only that, she'd seen the way guys treated me when we went out. And, though I'd never expressly said so, I thought Amanda knew I was jealous of her relationship with Rusty.

"We talked a lot, and Cam asked me all about my performing. I didn't even notice him at the wedding, but he heard me sing. And get this, he actually looked me up online and watched a bunch of my videos."

"Oh wow," she said with a smile.

"He told me he loved my voice."

"Well, who doesn't?"

"Thanks," I said with a laugh. "Most guys don't bother asking me anything about myself, but with Cam, it was like he already knew some stuff about me before he came over to talk. I like to think that's at least part of the reason he came over to meet me."

"And not just because you're beautiful for once," Amanda said gently.

My eyes suddenly welled up with tears. It wasn't just her words, it was the deep sincerity behind them.

"Yes," I said, wiping my eyes. "God, I feel like such a bitch when I say stuff like that. It sounds so awful. Poor me, I'm so pretty, guys won't leave me alone."

"It's not bitchy, Wilder. Not at all. I understand what you're saying. I mean, I certainly don't know from personal experience what it's like to be hit on all the time. But I do know you're not a superficial person. You don't want to be known as just a pretty face, and I don't blame you one bit."

"A pretty face is enough to catch a guy's interest, but it's not enough to keep it," I said bitterly, thinking of Danny. "So if all a man wants from me is physical stuff, he might as well walk away now instead of later."

Shaking my head, I switched the conversation from my whiny self-pity back to Cam. "It was strange. If anyone else had told me they'd looked me up online, I would have found it creepy, but it wasn't. Not with him. I don't know what it was exactly. Just something in the way he talked to me felt like he was taking me seriously. Like he wasn't just trying to get me in bed, even though that was where we ended up."

Amanda sighed softly, looking worried.

"Well, technically, it wasn't the bed. It was the floor."

"What?" she nearly yelled.

Holding up my hand, I said, "I'm getting ahead of myself here."

Amanda's eyes were still open wide, and I knew she wanted me to spill the tea already. All in good time. I wanted to tell the story right.

"We just had this amazing conversation. I loved talking to him. It felt so easy and so wonderful, you know? He told me he doesn't like showtunes," I said, smiling at the memory.

"And that's ... good?" she asked, understandably confused.

"Yes!" I shouted. "Because he wasn't bullshitting me. I can't tell you how many guys pretend to like every-thing I like because they think it will get me into bed faster."

"Gotcha." Amanda swirled the wine in her glass. "That

makes sense. It's great if you have things in common, but lying about it isn't gonna help anything."

"Right. And we do have some stuff in common it seems. Baseball for one."

"Yeah, I guess you do kinda like baseball."

"I do, but you know I'm more of a casual fan. But it's more than that. Cam works really hard to be the best pitcher he can be. I can totally relate to that."

"So he feels the same way about baseball as you do about singing."

"Exactly!" I said, toasting Amanda with my wine glass. I loved that my best girl understood me so well. That, and I was a bit tipsy. "The time went by so quickly while I was talking to him. It was all so wonderful that I just didn't want the evening to come to an end. But Rusty had to close up, and ... So he never said anything to you about any of this?"

Amanda shook her head. "I'm sure he knew you would want to tell me."

"Good point. So anyway, we went back to his place."

"And?" she asked, leaning forward, wineglass in hand.

"And he told me he wasn't looking for a serious relationship."

Amanda sighed irritably. "Of course he did. Once he got what he wanted."

She set her empty wine glass down on the end table and sat back in her chair.

"No, no. It wasn't like that. Not at all. Cam warned me ahead of time that he wasn't the type to ever want to settle down. And by ahead of time, I mean at the bar before we went back to his place. I'm telling you, that's one of the things I really like about this guy. He doesn't play games."

Amanda nodded, still looking unsure.

"I guess."

"Believe me, he was very careful to make sure I knew what I was getting into before we did anything physical. He made it clear he wasn't looking for anything serious."

"How do you feel about that?"

I let out a deep sigh. "It sucks. Like, really sucks. I felt like we had a real connection, you know?" Shaking my head, I added, "If guys only understood how important listening can be. Seriously. Just *listen* for once. I feel like he's the only guy who's ever done that. Not even Danny cared much about what I had to say, though I didn't realize it at the time."

"There were a lot of red flags with that guy, I guess. Much clearer in hindsight."

"Yup. I don't know. Talking with Cam, it felt so right. Like he really could have been The One. But I guess not."

Lucky, the sweet little Chesapeake Bay retriever, came over and put his head in my lap. He seemed to know I was sad.

"Oh, you are so sweet," I said, petting his precious little doggie head. "You are such a good boy."

Renner came over too, not wanting Lucky to get all the attention.

"You're a good boy too, you goober," I told him, managing to pet both fur babies at the same time. Once they had their fill of attention, they wandered off to lay down.

"You think Cam will change his mind? About wanting to be in a relationship?" Amanda asked.

"I don't know. That would be so amazing, but it seems dangerous to think about, you know? Like I can't let myself hope for something like that. And it's hard to imagine he would change his lifelong commitment to bachelorhood just for me."

"Why not?"

"There's only one reason a guy would want to be with me, Amanda."

"How can you say that? You don't really think that, do you?"

"My looks are the only reason any guy has taken any interest in me ever. Including Danny. That's why he went and screwed somebody else once the attraction wore off."

I *hated* how bitter I sounded, but that was how I felt. Being cheated on had destroyed my self-confidence. I wanted to be an independent woman, to rise above it all, but it was so hard. Danny's infidelity had been such a gut-punch.

Lucky came back and rested his head on my lap again. What an angel he was. There was no purer soul than that of a dog who knows you're hurting and wants to help.

"I know Danny's betrayal hurt you horribly," Amanda said. "He didn't deserve you. Trust me, there's somebody out there who will love you for who you really are. Believe me, I never thought it would happen for me either."

Amanda spoke the truth. Every time we went out, guys ignored her and bought me drinks. I hated that. The look of rejection on her face had torn my heart to pieces. On the rare occasions I took a guy home for the night, it was never one of the jerks who had mistreated Amanda.

I scritched underneath Lucky's ears and gave him some snuggles. Once he was satisfied I was okay, he trotted off to nap next to Renner again.

"It's so strange. Even after knowing Cam for such a short time, I feel like if anybody could love me for who I really am, it would be him. But he doesn't want to be with me. He said so."

"That's *not* what he said, Wilder," Amanda said. "He said he doesn't want to be with anybody. That's totally different."

"I guess." I sighed wearily.

"I get that you're worried about getting your hopes up. But still, don't give up on this thing between you and Cam yet, okay?"

"Okay."

"Now," she said, leaning forward. "Tell me all about the floor sex."

13

CAM

I had a pretty good outing on the mound today. Only gave up two runs and got the win. My two-seamer fastball was coming along nicely; I'd tested it out a few times during the game. Maybe Trace was right to have confidence in it.

Other than Trace, nobody on the team spoke to me much. I really had intended to try to apologize for trash-talking Baltimore when I first got here, but I hadn't found the right moment. Or the right words. And now it seemed like too much time had passed. I guess I was hoping it would all blow over, but so far it hadn't. A few random fist bumps and the occasional "good game" comment from some of the guys was all I was gonna get.

To his credit, Brady was cordial but cool to me. I doubted I would have been so gracious if he'd talked shit about my baseball performance the way I did to him.

I'd probably have punched him in the face.

I kept my cool most of the time, but I didn't have great impulse control when I was provoked.

After rinsing off in the shower, I got dressed and

prepared to head out. I mostly kept to myself in the locker room, not making eye contact with anybody before or after the game. My demeanor wasn't exactly the picture of friendliness, so I couldn't blame the guys for ignoring me for the most part. There were a few players who shot me hostile stares, probably members of the Brady Keaton fan club. Whatever. I was here to play baseball, not to make friends. I didn't really have friends on the Atlanta team either, but at least nobody hated me there.

As I headed for the door, I heard Brady joking around with Matt Jovey and Angel Jimenez. Those three seemed pretty tight. It was hard to imagine being close with any of the players, never mind hanging out with them in my free time. Once I made it to the New York team, I'd make some real friends there. Until then, as far as I was concerned, I was just passing through.

I walked through the tunnel under Old Bay Stadium and headed out to the fenced-in players parking lot. My thoughts turned to Wilder, as they often did in the few days since we'd had our first date, if you could call it that. Her phone number was burning a hole in my pocket. Or in my phone. Whatever. I'd been going back and forth on whether I should call her or text her or none of the above. After all, she hadn't actually given me her number.

But she had given me her body.

So there was that.

I stepped out of the tunnel into the light. It was an absolutely gorgeous evening. Gotta love a 3pm game time on a Saturday, because it left the evening free. Not that I had any special plans or anything. Normally, I would head to a local bar in search of a female companion for the evening. That was usually easiest when I pitched. Since I wasn't exactly famous yet, or at least I certainly wasn't Brady Keaton famous, it was kinda hit or miss that a woman recognized me. On game day, there was a better chance that they'd seen me on TV. It felt great when a woman's face lit up with recognition at a bar. I'd check for a wedding ring, and if I didn't see one, I was free to put the moves on her.

But not tonight.

I owed Wilder a phone call or at least a text after having had sex with her. I tried telling myself that was why I wanted to contact her, but it was bullshit. Well, mostly bullshit. I really was worried she might be hurt because we'd slept together and I hadn't called. But honestly, I wanted to hear her voice again. I wanted to see her. I wanted to be with her again, even if it was just to talk to her.

I stood next to my Harley with my phone in hand. I'd procrastinated enough over the last few days. I needed to just bite the bullet and contact the woman already.

A bunch of people gathered outside the fence started shouting. I looked up to see King Brady and his posse of Matt and Angel had emerged from the tunnel, much to the delight of all the Bay Birds fans. Brady headed over to the fence and started reaching for the baseballs and hats that people had brought for him to sign. I had to grudgingly respect the man. Most guys at his level of fame were too good to take the time for fans anymore. He did love this city and its fans, and they loved him right back.

"Great game, Cam," one of them shouted. I made the mistake of looking up and the guy added, "Now go the fuck back to New York where you came from."

I wish.

I guess winning ballgames wasn't enough to get the Baltimore fans to forgive me.

Just passing through, I reminded myself.

And now back to hemming and hawing about texting

Wilder. What were the odds she was free on a Saturday night at the last minute? For all I knew, she had a date. That thought made me feel slightly sick.

Another "fan" yelled some smartass remark at me. I didn't want to let on that these jerks were getting to me, but I also didn't feel like standing here and taking abuse all night. I took my time putting my motorcycle helmet on and putting my bag away in the bike's saddlebag. Finally, before hopping on my bike, I sent Wilder a brilliant text.

Hey Wilder. How's it going?

It took me four days to come up with that?

I revved up my bike and got the hell out of there.

The whole ride home, I kept glancing at my phone dock, hoping for a response. Nothing. But my apartment was only minutes away from the ballpark. Wilder's lack of response didn't necessarily mean anything.

But it could mean she was out on a date with some other guy.

Wilder Price was an extraordinarily beautiful woman. I'd never seen anyone as striking as her. Not in real life, anyway. Just on magazine covers and in the movies. Though her beauty was what had made me notice her in the first place, that wasn't what kept me attracted to her.

It was everything else about her.

The car behind me honked in annoyance, and I snapped to attention. I had no idea how long the light had been green while I'd been fantasizing about Wilder.

Breathing in the fresh air as I rode my bike home, I thought about how much I admired her. She was an insanely talented singer, and I could tell how bad she wanted to perform for a living. And she was very sweet. I loved the way she'd cared for Amanda at the wedding, and I remembered seeing her face light up with happiness for her friend. If Wilder was jealous of Amanda's happiness, she didn't show it much.

I arrived at my place, reluctantly parking my bike and trudging up to my apartment. What had I been expecting? A gorgeous woman like Wilder to just sit at home on a Saturday night? I'd been so worried about her being upset over our one-night stand and me not calling. But as it turned out, I was the one getting all butt hurt.

I couldn't help it. I really, really liked Wilder. And I wasn't sure what to do with that.

I flopped down on the couch, feeling like a loser alone on a Saturday night.

Then my phone buzzed in my back pocket.

Scrambling to yank it out, I dropped the damned thing. Cursing, I picked it up from the floor. The message was from Wilder.

"I am such an idiot," I said when I read it.

Wilder: *Sorry ... who is this??*

Of course she wouldn't know who it was; I'd gotten her number from Rusty. I thought about playing it cool and not answering for a while, but I was getting sick and tired of my own games. I wanted to be with her. As soon as possible.

Me: *Sorry. It's Cam. Rusty gave me your number. Hope that's okay.*

Wilder: *Of course!*

I grinned, happy with how quickly she'd responded.

Wilder: *Awesome game today. Way to get the win.*

I loved that she'd watched the game. Thank God I'd had a good outing. Some days were pretty ugly on the mound. The last thing I needed was for her to see me get my ass kicked.

Thanks, I responded. *Just got home from the stadium.*

Maybe she wouldn't think I was a loser for being home

on a Saturday night if she thought I was just tired from the game. I figured I might as well shoot my shot.

Me: *Don't suppose you're free tonight?*

I waited several excruciating minutes for her to respond.

Wilder: *No, unfortunately. I'm hanging out at Amanda's right now.*

She wasn't out on a date. I breathed a sigh of relief.

Wilder: *Gotta wait for the wine to wear off before I drive home lol.*

Me: *Well, I hope you're having a good time.*

Wilder: *I always do with my bestie!*

I hesitated for a while, unsure what to say next. I desperately wanted to see her again.

Wilder: *I really want to see you again.*

Yes! She beat me to it.

I wracked my brain trying to figure out what to say. The last thing I wanted was to get all mushy and stupid about my feelings. Gross. That just wasn't me. But at the same time, I needed to make damn sure she knew I wasn't just looking for another hookup. Not that I didn't want to have fabulous sex with her again, but that honestly wasn't my top priority.

Then I came up with the perfect plan. *You free for breakfast tomorrow?*

Suggesting breakfast for a second date certainly didn't imply pressure for sex afterward like dinner or drinks did. Hopefully, meeting earlier in the day would let her know I just wanted to see her again.

Wilder: *Sure, that should work.*

Me: *Perfect. I got a game at 1:05 so morning is best for me.*

There. It was clear breakfast just meant food and her company and that was all I expected. This time, anyway.

We chatted back and forth to decide on a place to go.

Once we had that settled, there was just one more thing to figure out.

Me: *I can pick you up if you want. Or we can meet there.*

Wilder: *You can pick me up.*

"Sweet," I said, letting out a breath of relief.

Me: *Are you okay with the motorcycle or do you want me to bring the car?*

Wilder: *Ooh the motorcycle would be fun!*

Just when I thought this girl couldn't get any cooler.

After a few more texts, including an awkward reminder that I didn't know where she lived, our plans were set.

WILDER'S PLACE was a rowhouse in downtown Baltimore that wasn't far from my apartment. It was a hassle to find parking on the street for my bike, but I finally got a spot about a block away. As I walked toward her place, it occurred to me that this quaint little neighborhood reminded me a lot of where I grew up in Brooklyn Heights, New York. Baltimore was like New York in that you could have a nice, low-key neighborhood on one street and then just a few streets over it was like a war zone.

I hoped Wilder was safe living here, but her street did seem pleasant. Nice, brightly colored row homes with freshly cut lawns. Kids playing outside and dads washing their cars. A few houses had Baltimore Bay Birds flags out front, which was cool. Naturally, there were a bunch of Maryland flags flying high as well.

I walked up the steps to Wilder's house and knocked on the door. After a few seconds, she opened the door with a smile.

Damn, this girl was gorgeous.

Her pretty, blond hair blew slightly in the breeze, and there was such a sweetness in her blue-green eyes. Wilder was hardly the first beautiful woman I'd slept with, but so far she was the only one who wasn't super hung up on her looks. Rather than show off how pretty she was, it was almost like she tried to hide it.

"Good morning," she said.

"It is now," I told her.

She laughed softly. "Come on in."

I entered the living room to see another pretty girl. A young woman with beautifully dark skin and incredibly pretty brown eyes looked up at me and smiled.

She got up from the couch. "So you're the baseball player."

"That would be me," I said, extending my hand to her.

"Cam, this is my friend and roommate, Kerry Jordan."

"Very nice to meet you," I said.

"You too."

"Kerry is an artist," Wilder said proudly. "She made every one of these incredible sculptures."

Wilder gestured at all the delicately sculpted animal figures that decorated the room.

"Oh wow," I said, eyeing up an especially detailed horse sculpture. I was no art critic, but this was beautiful. "These are amazing."

"Thanks," Kerry said with a warm smile.

She gave off some good vibes, that Kerry. I was usually a pretty good judge of character, and I found it comforting to know Wilder wasn't living alone in the house. Kerry seemed like good people.

"Ready to go?" Wilder asked.

I nodded, and we said our goodbyes to Kerry and headed out.

As we walked toward my bike, I fought the urge to hold Wilder's hand.

And that was *really weird* for me.

I was not the hand-holding type. But somehow, it would have felt comfortable with her.

For the briefest instant, it felt like we were a real couple. And not just a couple, but a husband and wife walking through the neighborhood where we lived.

The entire notion struck me as completely absurd. I shook my head as if to erase the image.

"You okay?" Wilder asked. I hadn't realized she'd been watching me.

"Uh ... yeah. Thought I felt a bug in my ear." I put my pinky in my ear like an idiot.

She nodded.

We reached my bike, and I relaxed. I felt the most like myself when I was riding my Harley, and I couldn't wait to share the experience with her.

I opened the trunk and pulled out the extra helmet for her.

"You ever been on a motorcycle before?"

"Yeah, a few times. My uncle has one, and he's taken me on a few rides. It's so much fun."

I was glad she hadn't said an ex-boyfriend had a motorcycle. I wanted this ride to be my thing with her, not memories of a past love.

I helped her secure her helmet, which also felt like a very "couply" thing to do. Only this time, I didn't try to shake off the thought. I kinda *liked* the thought.

Since I wasn't the type to date, I rarely took women out on the bike. Once in a while one of my hookups would request a quick ride—on the motorcycle that was—and I would oblige. But this was different.

Because Wilder wasn't just any woman.

Just having her grip my waist on the ride to the restaurant was a thrill, and I hoped she felt safe with me on the bike.

When we got to the brunch place, I pulled into a parking spot, got off the bike, and took off my helmet before helping Wilder with hers. Once it was off, she shook her blond hair like something out of the movies.

So. Damn. Pretty.

She smiled at me. We took a brief moment to look into each other's eyes before walking into the restaurant. Such a simple thing, but it seemed like everything took on greater meaning with her.

Since this place had a breakfast buffet, it wasn't long before we were settled at a table with coffee, orange juice, and plates full of food. It was nice sitting across from Wilder in a cozy booth, but I hated that I couldn't touch her.

Once things got quiet while we were eating, I felt I should say something about our first date.

"Wilder," I began awkwardly. "I just wanted to say ... ah ..." I had an idea of what I wanted to express, but not the actual words.

She eyed me curiously, a spark of amusement in her eyes.

"Ummm ... just that ..." I fumbled.

She laughed, but not in a mean way. "Just spit it out, Cam. What do you want to tell me?"

"I hope we didn't move too fast for you the other night," I said at last.

Wilder smiled, then sipped her coffee. "I'm a grown woman, you know. I can handle myself."

"I know, I know. I just ... wanted to make sure you were okay."

Lowering her voice to a respectable level for a family restaurant, she said, "Didn't I sound okay when I was screaming your name when you made me come?"

I sputtered with my orange juice, making her laugh.

"Fair enough, fair enough," I said, thrilled to know she'd had a good time with me. I felt a renewed urge to reach across the table and touch her, take her hand at least.

But I didn't.

"So I kinda feel like I'm doing all this backwards," I said, fiddling with my cloth napkin. "You know, sleeping with you first and then asking you more about yourself. But where do you work? What do you do?"

"I work at Weaver's Steak House as my so-called day job, though it's always in the late afternoon or evenings."

"That's a really nice place," I said, easily picturing Wilder working at a high-end establishment. "I've been there a few times. They have incredible food."

"They sure do, and they're really great to work for. Been working with them since I was in college. I started as a host- ess, and now I'm a bartender there."

"I guess you need that flexible schedule to go on audi- tions and stuff."

"Exactly," she said softly, seeming pleased I'd thought of that.

"So Wilder is a perfect name," I said. "A little too perfect."

"Too perfect? What does that mean?" She nibbled on her toast.

"Is it a stage name?" I asked, knowing damn well it was since Rusty had teased me about not knowing her real name.

"You got me," Wilder—or whoever she really was—said with a giggle. "Wilder is my mother's maiden name, so I kinda co-opted it. Started going by that name when I went to college. The perfect time to kind of reinvent yourself, you know?"

"So ..." I said.

"So what?"

"Spill it. What's your real name?"

She groaned.

"I would never disrespect you by actually calling you by your birth name, Wilder," I said sincerely.

"Thank you." She met my gaze. A jolt of renewed attraction zinged through my whole body when she looked at me like that. "My real name is Brianna."

"No, your *given* name was Brianna, which does *not* suit you. Your real name is Wilder."

"Yeah. You're right," she said with a definitive nod. "I like the way you think."

"It's cool you're a bartender at Weaver's. That place ain't cheap, and I hope those rich bastards tip you well."

"They do, for the most part," she said. "Good thing, because in addition to my rent and all the usual expenses, I still have student loans to deal with."

"It sucks your parents wouldn't pay for your degree," I said, getting pissed off just thinking about it. "It's one thing if they couldn't afford it."

"They have tons of money, believe me." She sighed. "But they insisted theater was a waste of time and money."

"But you went ahead and did it anyway. Good for you." I toasted her with my coffee.

"Thanks," she said with a smile that made my insides go all gooey again. "I'll be paying off my student loans for the rest of my life, but I'm not sorry. Definitely helps that I make pretty good money at the restaurant. And my boss is great about letting me have time off when I have an audition or rehearsals."

"Rehearsals? You do theater stuff around here I guess?"

"Oh yeah, all the time. Tons of community theater. Trying to pad up my resume as much as possible. Right now I'm in rehearsals for *Sweeney Todd*. They actually offered me the lead part, but this time I went for a lesser role so I could focus on preparing for my big *Beauty and the Beast* audition. The *Sweeney Todd* show starts in a few weeks."

"I'd love to see it," I said.

"That would be great." Those gorgeous blue-green eyes of hers lit up like they always did when she spoke about the theater. Damn, I loved this girl's passion. I could tell she was giving this performing thing everything she had, and I hoped like hell her dream would come true.

"I can't see the name Brianna Price in Broadway lights," I said, shaking my head. "But Wilder Price? Oh yeah. That's gonna happen."

Wilder got quiet, and I was afraid I'd said the wrong thing somehow.

"Do you really think so?" she asked after a moment of contemplation.

"Yes," I said with zero hesitation. I guess I didn't *know* she would make it to the Great White Way someday. But I did know she had the talent. And that she deserved to make it.

"You don't think it's crazy to actually think I could make it to Broadway?"

"Of course not. Why? Who tells you it's crazy?" I asked, my voice rising. I was ready to kick this unknown person's ass.

"My family sure does."

"Yeah, they'll do that," I said bitterly.

"I take it you know that from personal experience?"

"Oh, hell yeah. When I said I wanted to be a pro ballplayer, my parents laughed at me. Said that was like sayin' I wanted to be an astronaut or president of the United States."

"Well, you sure showed them." Wilder's smile was triumphant.

"I guess," I grumbled. "They sure had plenty to say when Atlanta dumped me."

Shit. I did not mean to bring that up. I wanted Wilder to think of me as a masterful pitcher on the mound, not some loser whose last team cut him loose.

Wilder gazed at me with sympathy, but her pity was the last thing I wanted.

"They were stupid to let you go," she said kindly.

I appreciated her words, but I wanted to change the subject ASAP.

"Just don't let anybody ever tell you that you can't do it. They don't know what the hell they're talking about."

"All I know is that I can't *not* do it. It's in my blood, you know?" Wilder said.

"Yes. I do know."

And I did.

"Maybe someday I'll make it to New York," she said.

I don't know what came over me, but I blurted out, "I'm going to New York with the team next week. You should come with me."

Wilder blinked. "What?"

I knew what I'd said was crazy, but what the hell? I doubled down.

"Yeah. Come with me. The team hates me anyway, so I might as well have a friendly face there with me for once. It's a three-game series, and I'm pitching on day three. We would have some time to sightsee, and we could stay at my place in Brooklyn Heights."

"Are you serious?" she asked, eyes wide.

"Sure, why not?"

"Cam, that would be *amazing!*" Wilder reached across the table and grabbed my hand, sending fresh lightning bolts of sheer desire through my body. Though my initial intentions had been pure—I wanted to take her to visit the city of her dreams—I couldn't help imagining having sex with her in my bedroom in New York. The sounds of her crying out my name in orgasmic bliss were still fresh in my mind.

I wouldn't pressure her, of course. But if it happened ... that would be cool.

"You think you can get off work?"

Wilder laughed with delight. "Lucky for me the owner of the restaurant is a *huge* Bay Birds fan. I'll have no problem once I tell him where I'm going and with who."

I grimaced. "You sure about that? I'm not exactly a fan favorite around here."

"It'll be fine," she assured me, squeezing my hands.

"I dunno ... maybe you should tell him you're going to New York with Brady Keaton."

She laughed again, looking happier than I'd ever seen her.

I put that look on her face.

Best thing I'd done since I set foot in Baltimore.

14

WILDER

Cam took the bus to New York because he needed to travel with the team. He gave me the choice of taking the train or a plane to get there. I'd never been on a train before, so I chose that option. We all left super early in the morning to arrive in New York at around noon. The team needed time to get settled before the 7:05 game time.

It turned out to be a wonderful trip. Having a few hours to sit back and relax was such a luxury, and the view from the train windows was so nice. Well, not all of it was nice. This was a trip from Baltimore to New York, after all, and we traveled past everything from green fields to some pretty sad and broken-down neighborhoods. I was reminded to be grateful for everything I had when I saw how some people lived in pretty desperate poverty.

Between auditions and rehearsals and working so much, I couldn't remember the last time I'd been able to rest. The train ride gave me a chance to read, eat lunch, and nap before we arrived in New York. It was heavenly.

It also gave me plenty of time to fantasize about

spending a few days with Cam. I had to be careful with that line of thinking, but I found it tough to rein myself in. It was all too easy to imagine myself as Cam's girlfriend. We just seemed to fit so well together. Falling into easy conversation, and the way his touch felt so right. Wrapping my arms around him on the motorcycle seemed so natural.

And yet Cam was hard to read. He hadn't said anything to indicate that he'd changed his mind about being in a relationship, and I knew better than to read too much into his invitation to New York. He'd just happened to be playing there with the team, and he knew how much I loved the city.

I couldn't help but be excited to stay at his house. Again, I knew better than to make too much of that and what it could mean. We'd already slept together. It would be silly for me to stay at a hotel after we'd been intimate.

Gazing out the window as we approached New York City, my body tingled all over. Visiting the Big Apple again and spending time with Cam Becker was equally exciting.

Especially since I'd decided I wanted to have sex with him again.

I did my best not to overthink whatever this thing was with Cam. His company was wonderful, and he was by far the best lover I'd ever had. I wanted to enjoy every moment of this for as long as it lasted.

Once the train arrived at the station, I took a cab to the hotel where the rest of the team was staying. I sat on a couch in the lobby with my luggage to wait; it wasn't long before the team's bus arrived. Brady spotted me first and walked over to me. I didn't know him well, but he was good friends with Rusty. He mainly knew me from the wedding since he was a groomsman.

"Wilder? What are you doing here?" he asked, his brown eyes full of surprise.

I stood up to talk to him. Good lord, was that man tall. Cam was only slightly shorter than him. Most of the ballplayers milling around the hotel lobby were larger than life.

"Cam Becker invited me to come with him on the trip. I'm staying with him in Brooklyn Heights."

Brady grimaced, which cracked me up. He clearly still was not a fan of Cam.

Giggling, I assured him, "Cam's a really great guy once you get to know him."

Brady's expression didn't change; he wasn't convinced.

"I know he's a little ... prickly sometimes. But I promise he means well. After all, he brought me here because he knows how much Broadway means to me."

"Huh," was Brady's response. "And that's the only reason he brought you here?"

"Well. Not the *only* reason." I said it in a way that made it pretty obvious Cam and I were hooking up.

"Oh." He looked more annoyed than ever. Then his expression softened. "Just be careful, okay?"

"What do you mean?"

"Cam just ..." Brady hesitated. "Look, I'm not trying to meddle in your personal business here. But ... you should know that when we're on the road, it's not unusual for him to bring girls back to his hotel room."

My heart sank. Brady looked almost as sad as I felt, clearly not relishing being the bearer of this news.

"I can't say that really surprises me," I said, forcing a smile. "He's been pretty upfront about not wanting to get into a serious relationship."

"Well, at least he's not lying to you. I'll give him that," he said. "I'll be around if you need anything, okay?"

His face took on a harder edge, and his meaning was

clear—he'd be happy to kick Cam's ass on my behalf should the need arise.

"Thanks," I told him. "I hope you have a great series against the Kings."

Brady nodded. "See ya around."

He went off to join his team and literally crossed paths with Cam, who looked a bit taken aback by the fierce stare he got from the usually affable Brady Keaton.

"I don't think he's happy you're here with me," Cam said as he approached me.

"No, he certainly is not. But I am happy to be here with you," I told him.

"Cool," he said with a smile. "Glad you made it here safe. How was your trip?"

"It was lovely. Being on the train was so much fun."

"Good. I've arranged for transportation for us to get to Brooklyn Heights. It's about a half hour from here."

"Nice." I reached for my luggage, but he grabbed it first.

My insides warmed at the gesture. With Cam, it felt like the little things were big things.

I followed him outside to find a sleek, black limo.

"Is that for us?" I asked, my eyes wide.

"Yes."

"Oh my gosh!" I yelled, totally uncool for New York. But it was hard to care.

I saw the twinkle in Cam's eyes; he was enjoying my reaction.

The limo driver stepped out of the car, dressed up all fancy in a tuxedo. He opened the limo door and helped me inside, making me feel like a famous movie star. Better yet, a Broadway star.

I sat on one of the long leather seats and Cam settled in beside me.

"This is amazing," I told him. Between the limo and having Cam sit so close to me, I was already having a wonderful time in New York.

The limo started to move, and I was torn between gazing at Cam and looking out the window at the city.

"I admit I'm not usually the flashy type," he said. "Normally I'd take an Uber or a cab to my house. But I thought this might be fun for you."

"It is, Cam. It is!" I chirped happily. He chuckled at my enthusiasm.

I turned to look out the window, taking in the tall buildings and the hustle and bustle of the crowded streets. As always, the traffic was heavy, so we weren't going anywhere fast. That was okay by me.

I wasn't sure how long I stared out the window, but eventually I became aware that Cam was watching me. I'd had lots of men stare at me, but as usual with Cam, it felt different. He wasn't ogling my breasts. He enjoyed watching me because he knew I loved being in New York.

At last, I tore my gaze away from the window to look at him.

I saw that familiar intensity in his brown eyes. It was the same look he had on the mound at Old Bay Stadium. Except now, that intensity was focused on *me.*

"Thank you for bringing me here," I said.

"You are so incredibly welcome." He caressed my cheek, gazing into my eyes. Then he leaned in and kissed me.

The moment was like a fairy tale. I felt like I was in Cinderella's carriage and the handsome prince, overcome with emotion, had given in to his passion and desire and indulged in kissing me. Cam's kiss was deep and passionate, his strong arms wrapped around me, engulfing me with his body.

He didn't kiss like he wasn't interested in a real relationship. He held me as if we were already in one.

This deep, wonderful, magical kiss lasted longer than any we'd shared that first night. Then again, we'd been driven by desperate sexual desire at his place. This time felt different.

This kiss felt like it meant more. Much, much more.

Eventually Cam released me, stroking my cheek one more time before letting go.

"I'm glad you're here," he said.

"Me too."

He sat back in his seat, and I couldn't help feeling like he was pulling back emotionally as well. As if he was second-guessing his choice to caress my face like a real boyfriend might.

I looked out the window again, but Cam didn't seem to mind.

"Have you been to New York before?" he asked.

"Oh yeah. But believe me, it's a thrill every time. It's so expensive that I usually do a day trip to go see a show or whatever. It's fun, but it makes for a really long day with all the travel."

"Damn," Cam said, shaking his head. "The bus trip up here was about all I could take today. Can't imagine having to drive back the same day."

I shrugged. "You do what you gotta do when you're broke."

He nodded thoughtfully, and I wondered what was going through his mind.

It was my turn to watch him as he gazed out the window. His expression was filled with as much longing as I felt.

"I really hope you get to play here someday," I said.

Cam's intense expression softened a bit. He didn't say

anything. He simply nodded. The trade to Baltimore instead of his hometown must have been really hard. I hoped with all my heart that he would get to wear a New York Kings uniform and represent his beloved team.

"And I look forward to seeing you perform on Broadway," Cam said confidently, as if it were a foregone conclusion.

"Ooh, that would be so amazing." I literally quivered with excitement at the thought. Cam chuckled at my enthusiasm. "What was it like growing up here?"

"Mostly I remember lots of yelling," he said, sounding unexpectedly bitter.

I shot him a quizzical look.

"My parents," he explained.

"Oh. Are they divorced?"

"Yeah."

"How old were you when they got divorced?" I asked.

"Fourteen. And they still hate each other. Believe me, holidays are a lot of fun," he scoffed.

"Oh, I bet they are."

"My mom and dad can't stand each other, and growing up it seemed all my friends' parents were the same way. I don't know why anyone would want to get married. All the husbands and wives I know make each other miserable."

Ah, another piece of the puzzle. At least Cam had valid reasons for not wanting to settle down.

"That's not true. What about Rusty and Amanda?"

"Give it time," he said gruffly.

"Cam!"

Chuckling deep in his throat, he said, "Sorry. Don't mean to be so cynical."

"I know lots of happily married couples. Like Brady and Lyric for one."

"Of course. Brady Keaton, King of Baltimore."

I laughed, detecting a hint of jealousy in his voice.

"I am sorry about your parents, Cam. That must have been really hard on you as a kid."

"It was. I don't have any brothers or sisters, so there was nobody to commiserate with, you know?"

I nodded, scared to make any sudden moves that might make him stop confiding in me. I figured it was probably good for him to get this stuff off his chest.

Cam paused, and I waited.

"Seems like it's the same story everywhere I go."

"What do you mean?" I asked.

"Like when I go on road trips. I'll go to a bar after a game, and there's tons of local guys sitting there drinking and avoiding going home to their wives. What's the point of getting married if you can't stand your wife?"

"That is sad," I said. I couldn't exactly commiserate because my parents got along fine. And yet I understood what he meant.

Cam got quiet, and I had the feeling he was done opening up. For now, at least.

I peered out the window again. We were out of the main part of the city, so the limo was finally able to pick up some speed. I drew in a deep breath, trying to get the courage to ask Cam the question that had been burning in my brain.

Turning to face him, I said, "Can I ask you something?"

"Of course."

"Is it true that you bring a lot of girls back to your hotel room when you're on the road?"

"Where did you hear—" Cam stopped, looking pissed. "Brady. Of course."

He'd seen me talking to Brady in the lobby and put two and two together.

"He was just looking out for me."

Cam gazed at me, taking his time to respond. Finally, he said, "Do I take women back to my hotel room on road trips? Yes. Have I ever invited one to come with me on a trip? No."

I thought about that for a moment.

"I can live with that," I said.

He nodded, seeming relieved by my response.

"We're almost there," he told me.

A fresh ripple of excitement went through me.

I very much looked forward to being alone with Cam Becker at his house.

15

CAM

The limo pulled up outside my townhouse in Brooklyn Heights. Wilder seemed excited to see my place, and I was thrilled to have her here with me. Often feeling out of place in Baltimore, I was glad to have a friendly face here on my turf. I was looking forward to showing her my home.

Especially the bedroom.

I wasn't sure if anything was gonna happen between us again, but I certainly hoped so. I planned to leave the whole sex thing up to her. I'd follow her lead wherever it went.

The limo driver helped Wilder out of the car, and I got out after them. After thanking the driver and tipping him well, I turned to Wilder.

She looked around the neighborhood in wonder, just like she'd looked at everything in wonder since she'd arrived in New York. It was freaking adorable.

"Wow, this is a really nice area," she said, glancing down the tree-lined street. "I've never been to Brooklyn Heights before."

"It's not bad." I was underselling it. I loved this neighborhood. Far enough from the noise of Manhattan, but not too far to miss out on the action of the city. That was another reason I hated being in Baltimore; I had to be away from my home. Most players had to stay in a different city during the season from where they lived, but some guys came from places that didn't even have a team. This was different. New York had a perfectly good baseball team not far from here, and that was where I wanted to play.

I led Wilder up the steps to my house and let her walk in ahead of me once I unlocked the door.

"I love your place, Cam," she said, her pretty eyes wide as she took in the living room that featured a leather furniture set, glass coffee table, and a big screen TV. The perfect place to relax during the off-season when I wasn't working out or traveling.

"Thanks," I said. I was proud of my place, and it felt so damn good to be home.

I took her downstairs to the finished basement to show off my bar, which had a ton of booze for mixed drinks and a tall beer fridge.

"There's a definite theme here," Wilder said with a laugh.

The theme was motorcycles. Harley Davidson, to be specific. My basement bar featured a glowing neon Harley clock, a large black and white framed Harley photo, and even the beer fridge sported the Harley logo.

"Sure is," I said proudly.

"This is definitely a man's house." She smiled over at me.

All I did was nod, but inside I was yelling and pumping my fist in the air. She'd just given me the perfect compliment, and I loved that she admired my home.

"All that's left now to see is the upstairs."

And the bedroom.

I hoped she'd have no issue sleeping in my bed with me, but again, I would follow her lead. If she seemed uncomfortable in any way, I'd give her the bed and I would sleep on the couch.

After showing her the hall bathroom so she could freshen up, we finally got to my bedroom.

As with the rest of the house tour, I paused to let Wilder look around. She glanced at the bed—queen-sized, with a silky black comforter. Then she gazed at the framed photograph of Charles "Chazz" Hunter, my favorite Kings pitcher from when I was a kid. She looked at it for a while, as if somehow she knew what the guy had meant to me, even though I'd never mentioned him to her.

While she was looking around, I tried to think of a delicate way to ask about the sleeping arrangements. She seemed a bit tired; she'd traveled a long way today. I wasn't pitching tonight, but I needed to be at the ballpark by 5:30 at the latest. It wasn't quite 2pm yet, so we still had some time. Still, Wilder might need to get some rest, so we needed to figure out the logistics of staying here together.

I was still figuring out how to broach the subject when Wilder sat down on the bed, looked up at me, and said, "So what do you think? Should we try it on the bed for once instead of the floor?"

So help me, I almost laughed. It was just so unexpected.

But hell yeah, I was on board with the idea.

"Don't have to ask me twice," I said, wasting no time in pushing her onto her back on the bed.

Wilder bit her lip as she looked up at me, her eyes flashing with excitement. Clearly, my earlier obsessive worry about us moving too fast was misguided. Wilder wanted this. Again. No doubt about it.

I kissed her mouth roughly, making her moan. As I

kissed down her neck toward her breasts, she kept murmuring my name in her sexiest, most seductive voice. It made me crazy. I loved it.

Being in my own home on top of this beautiful, talented, and incredible woman in my bed sent a surge of adrenaline through my body.

In no time, I'd stripped her of her blouse and bra and begun sucking on her breasts.

"Oh God, Cam," she moaned, tugging at my shirt. "I want this off."

"Done." I practically tore it off.

Wilder drew in a deep breath as she stared at my chest. Many women had stared at my chest, but her approval of my body meant more than ever before. I waited until her eyes traveled south, then I rolled off her to unzip my pants. Feeling her watch me, I slid my jeans and underwear off. I was rock hard already. She sucked in another breath of anticipation.

I sat up and quickly rid her of her pants and lacy underwear.

"Mmmm, I like these," I said, fingering her black panties before tossing them aside.

What I *really* liked was that she'd worn a matching set of black bra and panties as if she'd planned to have sex with me.

Wilder looked positively *delicious* lying completely naked on my bed. I grabbed her ankles and opened her up wide. She gasped.

I fucking love the way she gasps every time I do something that turns her on.

My eyes bored into hers while I made her wait, still holding her legs wide open.

"I need you, Cam," she pleaded.

"I'll give you what you need," I told her firmly. "Be patient."

After waiting a few more seconds, I teased her clit with the tip of my cock.

"Oh ... God ..." she said, and I watched her eyes roll back in her head.

I rubbed her more ... And then a little bit more ...

"Oh ... oh ..." Wilder panted. She gripped the black comforter tightly in her hands. Just watching her pleasure grow stronger was so ... fucking .... hot.

I pulled my cock away, and her eyes opened wide in protest. Her need must be agonizingly painful by now. As was mine.

I crouched between her legs and tongued her, making her scream my name. I remembered exactly how she liked it. Using the perfect rhythm, I swirled my tongue faster and faster until she gripped the sheets and cried out my name again in ecstasy when she came.

When I sat up, she put her hand on her forehead, still panting heavily. Her legs literally quivered.

In a weak voice, she said, "I've never ... come that hard ... in my life."

Sweet.

I resumed my original position, grabbing her ankles and opening her up. Wilder's sleepy, satisfied blue-green eyes met mine. She bit her lip again and said seductively, "Go to it, baby."

Good thing because I was about ready to explode.

I rammed into her and she cried out, wrapping her arms around my neck. I pounded in and out of her *hard.* As always, Wilder was super into it. Moaning my name and gripping my back.

I felt so connected to Wilder when we had sex. I mean, it

was impossible to be physically closer to another person while you were doing it, but this emotional part I wasn't used to. She gazed up at me with those darling eyes as if she enjoyed my pleasure as much as I'd enjoyed hers.

It didn't take long to find my release. Letting out a deep groan that was more like a growl, I shuddered hard as I came. Sex with Wilder was completely, utterly satisfying. Emotionally, physically, and whatever else there was. I'd never felt closer to anyone. Maybe it was the explosive orgasm talking, but I didn't think so.

Damn, we were good together.

In every possible way.

Wilder let out a deep, hopefully happy sigh as I rolled off her. Instinctively, I pulled her into my arms as we lay together in bed.

Whoa.

That was normally *not* my after-sex instinct. I was hardly the cuddler type. Not only was I uncomfortable with that kind of intimacy, but I never wanted the woman I was with to get the wrong idea. As with Wilder, I'd told every woman I'd been with that I wasn't looking for anything serious.

And now? I had no idea what I wanted anymore.

All I knew was that ever since I met Wilder, I'd been questioning my goal of lifelong bachelorhood.

It was weird.

And kinda awesome.

"You know how I told you I bring girls back to my hotel room when I'm on a road trip?" I said suddenly.

Wilder winced. "Yeah. I'm kinda wondering why you're bringing it up *now*."

"I'm not gonna lie and say I haven't been with a fair number of women ..."

Her body tensed, still pressed up against mine.

"But I want you to know I've never brought a woman back here. Ever. My house is my sanctuary. Believe it or not, I've never even had sex in this bed with anyone until now."

I felt her tense muscles relax, which made me relax. I worried about screwing things up with her by saying the wrong thing.

"Really?" she asked quietly.

"Yeah. I just ... wanted you to know."

"Thanks for telling me that, Cam," she said, snuggling even closer to me.

In that moment, I felt a sense of calm I'd never experienced before in my life.

Oh yeah.

I could get used to this.

16

WILDER

The next morning we headed back to Manhattan, by Uber this time. The drive was every bit as much fun as the limo ride had been.

I was in the city of my dreams with the man of my dreams. Still, I rather wished he would put his arms around me or something, especially since this car was so much smaller and cozier than the limo. It seemed like a natural thing to do, but then again, maybe that was a little too "boyfriendy" for his comfort.

It was still risky to think of Cam in boyfriend terms. After all, he hadn't told me he'd changed his mind about settling down. But there were some subtle signs.

Confessing that I was the only woman he'd ever had in his bed at home was a big one. He didn't have to tell me that, but he'd clearly wanted me to know. I wasn't about to push the whole relationship thing, though. The last thing I wanted was to scare him off, but at least I had reason to be optimistic.

"Of course we can go anywhere you want in the city," Cam said. "But there's one place I want to take you first."

"Okay," I said, feeling excited. I didn't ask him where we were going because he seemed to want it to be a surprise. I figured it would be some cool local spot he knew about as a native New Yorker.

"And we should have time to catch a matinee of a Broadway show before I have to be at the ballpark tonight."

Cam had gotten me tickets to tomorrow night's game, when he was pitching. Tonight, I was on my own in New York, which would also be fun.

"What show do you want to see?" he asked.

"Well, I guess it all depends on what we can get tickets for at the last minute," I said.

"No it doesn't."

"What?"

"I can get tickets to whatever you want, Wilder. Just name the show."

"You can? How can you do that?"

Cam hesitated to answer, and for a moment I was concerned he might be hiding something.

"You're not connected to the mob, are you?" I asked. I was only half-joking.

Cam burst out laughing, something I'd never seen him do.

"Of course not." After a moment, he explained. "Money, Wilder. I have lots of money. Enough to easily get two tickets to whatever show you want."

I nodded thoughtfully. "You don't like talking about being rich, do you?"

Cam gazed at me. He seemed grateful that I understood.

"No, I don't. I came from sort of humble beginnings. Not poverty or anything. I just had a normal upbringing, I guess, and it feels kinda weird to be paid so much money for playing ball. Believe me, I'm nowhere near the top-level kind of athlete or anything. That would be Brady Keaton for sure."

Cam seemed to compare himself to Brady a lot, which wasn't a good idea. Brady was a superstar. Very few athletes ever reached that crazy level of fame.

"The occasional limo ride aside, I really don't like showing off my wealth."

"I think that's pretty cool, Cam," I told him.

I was surprised when we got to our destination.

"Times Square? Really?" I asked, unable to hide my shock. Far from an out-of-the-way local spot, Times Square was the most touristy place in New York. And maybe the most touristy place in the whole country.

"I know, I know," he said with a glint in his eye. "Trust me."

Cam helped me out of the car. As I looked around at the throngs of people crowding the streets, I couldn't help but feel disappointed. That was, until he clued me in on his plan.

"Here we are," he said, gesturing to my right to a large building.

"Ohhh," I said with a laugh.

Cam had brought me to the Disney Store in Times Square.

Chuckling, he said, "I know it's a chain store, and I know you've no doubt been here before."

I nodded. Of course I had. I *loved* Disney.

"But I know you love Disney," Cam said, proving how well he knew me already. "And though I meant it when I said I don't like showing off how much money I have, I want you to go in and pick out whatever you want."

"Cam," I protested.

"Whatever you want," he said so firmly that it made me jump. "Just ... please let me do this for you. Okay?"

I pulled him in for a kiss, and he eagerly returned it.

He led me into the store. "After this," he said, "I'll take you someplace cool for lunch, okay?"

"Oh yeah, where? Pizza Hut? The Cheesecake Factory? TGI Friday's?" I teased.

"Very funny. I'll take ya someplace local. I promise."

Giggling, I said, "Cool."

I watched Cam's eyes glaze over with boredom as he scanned the huge Disney Store filled with brightly colored toys, clothes, and every kind of movie and cartoon merch you could imagine. It was kind of hilarious. And very sweet that he'd brought me to a place he clearly hated.

"I won't take long, I promise."

"Take all the time you want. Oh hey, while you're here, I'll go get the tickets for the show. You never did tell me which one you wanted to see."

"Six," I responded with no hesitation.

"Six?" he asked, clearly having never heard of the show. Damn, he really had zero interest in musicals. He lived in New York and the signs for the show were everywhere, and yet he was clueless. "As in one, two, three, four, five, six?"

Laughing, I said, "Yes. Just *Six.*"

He shrugged. "Okayyy. Easy enough to remember, I guess. I'm on it. Be back soon."

Cam headed out to the streets to work whatever non-Mafia magic he had to conjure to get last-minute tickets to the popular show. I wandered around the store, my stomach bubbling with excitement about being in New York. I figured *Six* was the perfect musical for the non-musical type like Cam. The music was closer to pop than traditional showtunes, but I still loved the show. Not that I'd seen it yet, but I knew all the songs by heart. A relatively short musical with no intermissions, it was the best choice for Cam. The number six referred to Henry the VIII's six wives, so the show was anything but the kind of gooey love story I figured Cam would hate. Instead, it was a pretty high-energy, peppy show. He would love it.

Well, he wouldn't *hate* it at least.

I headed to my favorite section, *Beauty and the Beast,* hoping *it* was still there. Cam had no way of knowing I visited the Disney Store every time I came to New York and always drooled over this absolutely stunning glass figurine of Belle and the Beast at the castle. Delicate, with intricate glass etching, I loved it. But the damned thing was five hundred dollars. I didn't care how much money Cam had, I had no intention of letting him buy me something so extravagant. After my customary visit with my figurine, I'd go pick up something much cheaper.

And there it was, behind the mirrored glass case as always. Staring at the beautiful, magic glass castle, I got lost in my imagination.

"I see you found something you like," Cam said.

Damn. I must have lost track of time. I hadn't wanted him to know this expensive glass castle existed. He knew how much I loved *Beauty and the Beast,* so if he'd stumbled upon it on his own, he probably would have bought it for me.

"Oh, Cam. This is far too expen—"

"Too late!" he exclaimed. "Wilder, I saw the way you looked at that thing. We're not leaving without it. And I got *Six* tickets by the way. I mean, I got *two* tickets to *Six.* Now let's get the castle thing wrapped up and we'll go to lunch."

Cam turned on his heel and headed to the register, and I

knew there was no arguing with him. That man was amazing.

This whole trip was positively *surreal*. Talk about a fairy tale. So far I'd been in a limo, had fabulous sex with a gorgeous man, was headed to a Broadway show, *and* would be going home with the *Beauty and the Beast* castle that I'd visited like a museum piece for years. This was crazy.

"Wilder!" Cam called over to me, snapping me out of my reverie. "Let's roll, already. Got a lot to do."

"Coming, coming," I said, practically stumbling over my own feet.

Cam took me to a lovely local bistro for lunch. The dimly lit restaurant was rather romantic, even in the daytime. We shared a charcuterie appetizer and homemade vanilla cheesecake in addition to our entrées. I hadn't eaten so much in one sitting in quite a while, but I figured I should indulge while I was on vacation.

I literally squealed with excitement as we got into the cab to head to the Lena Horne theater. I was just too excited to even pretend to be cool about going to a Broadway show. I'd only seen a handful of them in New York in my life, and it was a thrill every time.

When we got inside the theater, we kept walking down, down, down the steps until we were only a few rows back from the stage.

"Wow," I exclaimed as we sat. "I've never sat this close to a Broadway stage. I'm always waaaaay up there." I gestured toward the cheapest seats in the house.

"Well, just think. Someday you'll get even closer," he said with that sexy, side-of-his-mouth grin. "Someday you'll be up there."

He pointed at the stage. My stomach tingled just

thinking about it. I wanted it so damn much, but sometimes it was hard to imagine.

"Thank you," I said. "For everything."

I pulled him toward me and held him close. I expected him to pull away; I always expected him to pull away. But he didn't. Instead he took a deep breath, as if breathing me in.

Once I let go, I said, "This is all so wonderful, Cam. I'm loving every minute of being here with you."

He didn't respond. Not with words, anyway. Cam simply nodded, but there was a tenderness in his eyes that made me believe he felt the same way.

"I really think you're gonna like this show."

He chuckled, looking skeptical. "Anything's possible, I suppose."

I laughed. As always, I appreciated his honesty. He was more than happy to spoil me rotten while we were in New York, but he hadn't pretended to love the Disney Store, nor that he couldn't wait to see a Broadway musical. I loved that about him. Cam didn't have a fake bone in his body.

His reaction during the performance was hysterical. He'd come to this show without knowing the first thing about it, and I stifled a laugh at Cam's confusion at the show's opening words.

"Divorced." "Beheaded." "Died." "Divorced." "Beheaded." "Survived."

I could practically hear Cam thinking *what the fuck?*

But then the music kicked in, and the lyrics of the first song, "Ex-Wives" explained that the six women were Henry the VIII's wives. Cam nodded slightly, and he seemed on board with the story once he understood the premise.

I kept sneaking looks at him during the show only to find him doing the same with me. He seemed to relish watching me, and I loved being able to share my life's passion with him. *Six* had been an excellent choice; it featured a lot of humor and heart, as well as numerous fun, upbeat, and catchy songs.

There were also some emotional songs in the show, and for stretches of time, I got so caught up that I nearly forgot Cam was there. I even teared up a few times, both at the emotion of the show and just because I was there. Broadway always had that effect on me.

Six was a fast-moving show without a dull moment, which was perfect when you were dragging along a reluctant participant like Cam. Each wife had their own song about their lives, basically trying to win the contest of who had suffered the most because of the king. It was certainly tough to argue with the ones who'd been beheaded. I knew every word to every song, which made it even more fun for me. It was hard not to sing along, but I resisted.

I could hardly wait for the finale. The last song featured the women abandoning their connection with old Henry and singing about themselves instead. In productions of *Six* in other countries, fans were encouraged to record the finale on their phones so they could share their videos online. It had become kind of a cult following thing. Unfortunately, there were union rules in the United States that forbade it here. Still, it would be a thrilling end to a great show.

And it was.

For the finale, the crowd got to its feet. Oh, how I *loved* when a show ended on such a high note like that. I even pulled Cam up from his seat, and by the end he was clapping along. It was so un-Cam-like. And it was so damn cute.

I was all keyed up after the show, but in a good way. Too bad Cam had to get to the ballpark, because I could think of some pretty fun ways to work off all my extra energy.

"That was so freaking amazing, Cam," I said as we walked down the streets of New York after the show.

"You know what? It wasn't bad. It really wasn't," he said.

"So you admit you actually liked it?"

Glancing at me, he said, "I did, Wilder. I really did."

Then he chuckled.

"What?" I asked.

"It's just funny to see how energized you get after a show," he said.

"Oh yeah. Tons of energy for sure. That's what sucks about living in a townhouse. Not like I can belt out show-tunes at the top of my lungs as often as I'd like."

"I never thought about that. So where do you practice for auditions?"

"Fortunately, my old college in Towson lets me use their theater space for stuff like that. You know, when they're not using it. It's great. It's incredibly cathartic to go there and just belt out my songs. I love it."

"I bet. Probably the same way I feel when I'm throwing a fastball as hard as I can."

"Probably," I said with a smile. This man got me. He really did.

"I've been getting pretty good with my two-seamer fast-ball lately. Can't wait to try it out tomorrow."

"You must be excited to play at Kings Park."

"It's uh ... Well, it's bittersweet."

"I get that," I told him. And I did. He would be playing against his hometown instead of playing for them. That would be hard.

My Uber showed up, and Cam helped me inside.

"You go get some rest, okay?" he told me.

"I will," I said, reluctant to part ways after such a perfect day. Cam needed to get to the ballpark, so I was headed back to his place. He'd offered to let me run around New York with his credit card, but I'd declined. The man had been generous enough already.

"See you at home," he said.

See you at home.

Not see you at my place or simply see ya later.

Wow.

If this wasn't a real relationship, I wasn't sure what was.

17

———

CAM

On our third day in New York, it was finally my turn to pitch. Stepping out of the clubhouse and into the late evening sun, I drew in a deep breath, taking a moment to count my blessings.

I was standing on the field at Kings Park, the field of my dreams, as a Major League Baseball player. I spent way too much time bitching about not playing for my home team instead of appreciating how far I'd gotten. There were plenty of ballplayers who were every bit as talented as I was who would never make it here. I was convinced that success was a mix of talent, hard work, devotion, and luck. I knew damn well there were lots of guys who had all of that stuff and *still* would never make it. Life was scary that way. Good or bad, you never knew what was gonna happen on any given day.

I took a moment to look around at the stadium that was slowly filling up with fans. Gazing out at the field, a shiver of excitement went through me.

My God, the *history* here. Ten-year-old me would be proud, even if I was wearing the wrong uniform.

"Nothing like playing on your home field, huh?" came a voice from beside me.

It was Brady, clearly offering me an olive branch. No wonder it was impossible to hate that guy.

"Got that right," I said, offering him a small smile.

Brady nodded. He stood beside me for a moment. Then he clapped me on the back and walked away.

He really was a class act. Made me feel bad for acting like such a little bitch since I'd arrived in Baltimore. I took another minute or two to take in the atmosphere, like I always did when I had the privilege to play here. Then it was time to get to work.

As exciting as it was to pitch in this stadium, it was also pretty nerve-wracking to play in my hometown. Everything took on deeper meaning here. That, and it was Wilder's first time in the stands.

Yeah. A lot was riding on this.

Trace was catching me, of course. Before the game we'd settled on a mix of different pitches for my New York debut as a Baltimore Bay Bird. I'd been working hard on mastering my two-seamer. My goal was to become a real power pitcher like Justin Verlander, who had mastered the control and high velocity necessary to make the two-seamer a truly formidable pitch.

So I tried out my two-seamer on the mound at Kings Park.

Turned out I didn't have as much control over it as I'd thought.

I walked the first two batters. As a pitcher, there's nothing worse than looking for your first out when you're struggling. You get that horrible flop sweat, worried you're gonna walk the whole goddamned starting lineup. Trace flipped up his mask to make eye contact with me, trying to help settle me down. We were pretty in sync most of the time, and his gesture helped.

I managed to get the next two batters out after abandoning my clunky two-seamer that was obviously not ready for prime time. Instead, I relied on my regular fastball. My luck with that one ran out quickly; the next guy launched the ball into the stratosphere.

I got the next player out, but the damage was done. Just like that, the Birds were down 3-0.

The Kings pitcher made quick work of the Bay Birds. Three up, three down, and all too soon it was my turn again.

The second inning was better for me.

I only gave up *two* runs this time.

After I managed to load the bases in the third inning, the skipper yanked me. The crowd booed and mocked me. As well they should. New York sure as hell lets you know if you suck.

The walk of shame from the mound to the dugout would probably go down as the most humiliating moment of my life. Not that I hadn't had rough outings before. I'd been a ballplayer for years and years. Shit happens. But *this* shit happened in New York, in front of Wilder, and with most of my team still hating me and probably thrilled to see me eat it in front of thousands of fans.

It fucking *sucked.*

The Birds lost the game by five runs—the ones I'd given up.

Understandably, I got a chilly reception in the clubhouse. Everybody had a bad night from time to time, and the guys were usually supportive. Lots of claps on the back and shoulder punches, that kinda thing. *If* they liked you. The guys pretty much ignored me. Brady avoided my gaze like he was embarrassed for me, which made me feel even worse.

Pete Cristal, one of our outfielders, was the first to speak to me after the game.

"You hate playin' for Baltimore so much. Keep pitchin' like that, you won't have to worry about it for long, asshole," Pete spat at me.

Trace did clap me on the shoulder. "Tonight's not your night. It happens, man."

But why *tonight*? I wanted to yell and punch the wall.

Why did I have to get thoroughly shellacked in New York and in front of Wilder?

I got the hell out of there as fast as possible. Which wasn't all that fast, considering I had to wait for the damned Uber. Times like this I really missed my bike.

Worst of all, I had to face Wilder.

I texted her and told her where to meet so we could ride home together.

"Hey," was all she said when we met up near the players' parking lot gate. Wilder's eyes were filled with worry, but I think she knew better than to say much to me. My demeanor didn't exactly invite conversation.

In fact, I didn't say a word to her the entire ride home. I felt bad about it, but I just didn't have the mental energy to make small talk. Even with her.

Up until now, I'd really been in my element on this trip. Being in my own home, knowing all the local places, and being able to spoil Wilder the way she deserved made me feel in control in a way I hadn't since I'd been shipped off to Baltimore. Now I was sorry I'd brought her here to witness my humiliation.

No. I wasn't sorry.

I remembered the way she gazed up at the Broadway

stage, her face filled with awe, and the way her eyes filled with tears at an especially poignant song in the show. The way she looked at the *Beauty and the Beast* castle like it was the most wondrous thing she'd ever laid eyes on. No, I had no regrets about bringing her here.

"You okay?" she finally asked when our Uber got close to my place. I growled in response instead of using actual words. She nodded and went back to looking out the window.

Once we got back home, I turned to her where we stood in the living room.

"Wilder, I'm sorry. I'm not ... pleasant after an outing like that."

"I understand," she said, and the soft kindness in her eyes showed she had no hard feelings. Wilder did not expect me to be a great host right now, and I appreciated that. "I'll give you some space."

"Thanks. I'll probably just go down to the basement and have a drink or two before I come to bed."

"Okay." She kissed me on the cheek and walked away. "Can I just say one thing first?" she asked, turning back.

"Of course."

Looking me directly in the eye, Wilder said, "I know how you feel."

There was a slight tremor in her voice and the sheen of tears in her eyes. And I knew—really *knew*—that she did understand how I felt. No matter how ugly my loss was today, Wilder didn't think I was a loser. She knew the heartbreak of giving your dream everything you had and still it wasn't enough.

She walked upstairs to let me wallow in misery alone because it was the kindest thing to do for me right now.

18

WILDER

Ever since we got back from New York I'd been super busy with rehearsals for my local community center production of *Sweeney Todd,* preparing for my all-important *Beauty and the Beast* audition that was fast approaching, and working at the steak house. It had been hard to find time to see Cam, but I followed his progress with the Bay Birds religiously. He'd been pitching better than he had in New York, thank goodness. Watching him struggle like that had been torture for me. Times like that there was just nothing you could do to make things better. It was horrible. We texted each other a lot and occasionally spoke on the phone, but it wasn't the same as seeing each other in person. Sometimes I wondered if he missed me as much as I missed him.

The day of the big audition finally came, and I woke up feeling like death. I was really dizzy and thought I was gonna throw up. I legitimately believed I was sick until some seltzer water soothed my stomach and my nerves. Damn, I never got this worked up before an audition. If I didn't calm the hell down, I wouldn't have a prayer of getting the part.

Sitting at the kitchen table, I drew in a few deep, steady breaths. I had a real shot at getting my dream role, and I needed to remember that. After all, the only reason I'd gotten this opportunity was because they liked the video audition I'd sent them. Not everyone would even get this far. I did my best to gather my confidence based on that fact.

I forced myself to eat breakfast because I'd need sustenance to get through this marathon of a day. Still, eating was the last thing I wanted to do right now.

There was just so damn much riding on this one audition. This could be the big break I'd waited for all my life. The one that would make my dreams come true. The one that would show my family I wasn't just some wannabe Disney princess with her head in the clouds.

I thought back on all the lead roles I'd had in the past, still trying to build up my confidence. I'd even landed the lead role of Mrs. Lovett in *Sweeney Todd,* but I'd turned it down. I'd opted to play the lesser role of Johanna instead so I could devote more time to getting ready for my big audition.

As I sat at the kitchen table, I realized that overthinking was probably the worst thing I could do. Getting too inside my head would really mess me up, but it was hard not to. Though I often landed the lead in community theater productions, I couldn't help thinking that only meant I was a big fish in a small pond. Plenty of women at this audition would be every bit as talented as I was, and some probably more so.

Just as my confidence seemed to plunge into freefall, my phone buzzed with a text.

Cam: *You fucking got this. Give 'em hell, Belle.*

My heart melted and my tension eased. How thoughtful he was to remember today was my audition. His sweet message was so what I needed right now. A few minutes later, Amanda also texted with her love and support.

I was relieved when it was finally time to head to the rehearsal space in downtown Baltimore. It was better than sitting around stressing and worrying about it.

Kerry walked into the living room just as I was getting ready to walk out the door. She rushed over and hugged me.

"You're gonna crush this, baby. I know it."

"Thank you. Thank you so much," I said, squeezing her tight. Kerry was a fellow creative, and she knew what it was like to put your heart and soul on the line for your art. She was such a dear friend.

Armed with my months of preparation and the support of my friends, I headed out to do my best to "give 'em hell."

EVERY MOMENT LEADING up to the audition was excruciating. Waiting forever, sizing up the competition of beautiful and talented women, worrying if I was hydrated enough, and scared to death I was gonna throw up. During all that time, I'd failed to remember one crucial thing about auditioning —that once I got up onstage and started singing, all the anxiety and fear and madness always melted away. I was in my element onstage. It was where everything made sense, and *nothing* was more cathartic than singing my heart out, no matter who was watching or how important any audition was to my career. Onstage, I *became* the character and got lost in the words and the music.

I began my audition by singing "There's a Fine, Fine Line" from *Avenue Q*. Though it was essentially a song about unrequited love and represented a rare serious moment in a musical that was essentially about X-rated puppets of all things, the song had some lyrics I truly loved. My favorite part was about how important it was to go after the things you want while you're still in your prime. Standing on the stage, belting out my solo, that was exactly what I did.

The decision-makers at auditions are notoriously hard to read, but they did ask me to sing a song from *Beauty and the Beast* next. If they had no interest in me, they'd have moved on to the next singer. They had me sing "Home," which was fine by me. I knew every note of every song from the show. I could have done the entire thing solo if they'd asked me.

I crushed that song too, or at least I was pretty sure I did. They thanked me for my time, and then it was over.

I walked out of the large audition space on shaky legs and out into the humid, summer sun. Letting out a deep sigh of relief, I smiled. I'd done everything I possibly could to nail the audition, and there was nothing left now but to wait.

Still filled with adrenaline, I walked around Baltimore for a while, despite the heat. I figured soon enough I'd be starving, but I needed to burn off some of my nervous energy first. Walking along the Harborplace waterfront, my thoughts turned to Cam. I wondered what it would mean for us if I did get the part. I'd be traveling all over the country for months on the tour, which meant we'd barely see each other. As close as Cam and I had become lately, I felt like my grasp on him was tenuous at best.

I supposed if we were meant to be, my absence wouldn't change that. I just wished he would make some kind of formal commitment if he was serious about me. Not like I was looking for a ring or anything. Honestly, as much as I wanted to get married someday, the idea scared the hell out of me. What happened with Danny really messed me up. I couldn't help thinking it was only a matter of time until Cam got bored with me anyway, and being away for most of the next year if I got this part? Forget it. He'd probably replace me with a bunch of girls he met on the road.

Shaking off those sad thoughts, I figured that was a worry for another day. I was proud of the work I'd done at my audition, and I wanted to hold on to the feeling.

As luck would have it, my stomach started grumbling just when I got close to Power Bar and Grill. No better place to stop in for a bite to eat and get out of the heat for a while.

19

CAM

As much as my performance in New York sucked donkey balls, it turned out to be just a one-off. My next mound appearance in Toronto was a hell of a lot better. I missed Wilder so much while I was away. I also missed having sex on a regular basis; I no longer had any interest in sleeping with random women on road trips. Wilder was the only woman on my mind, and a couple weeks without her felt like a lifetime. Talking to her on the phone helped, but it wasn't the same as being able to look into her eyes.

After a long road trip, it was great to be back home. Well, back at Old Bay Stadium, anyway. Baltimore wasn't my home and never would be.

My first game back after the road trip went even better than the one in Toronto. I had an exciting no-hitter going through the third inning. I was finally getting more control over my two-seamer, and it was breaking nicely over the plate for once. I pitched through the seventh inning, which was awesome. Getting pulled from the mound because you've reached a high pitch count was so much better than being yanked because you sucked.

The Birds held on to their 4-1 lead for the rest of the game, so I got the win. After the game, I changed into my street clothes and headed out. A few of the guys even congratulated me on my way out. Slowly but surely, I was gaining acceptance. That was pretty cool, I guess, especially since I'd never apologized for all the shitty things I'd said about Baltimore. These fellas were more forgiving than I would have been. I'd give them that.

I glanced at my phone as I walked through the tunnel toward the parking lot. There was a text message from Wilder.

Damn, you looked great out there tonight.

I grinned at my phone, thrilled to know she'd been watching me kick some ass after my horrific appearance in New York.

Wilder: *Can I catch a ride home with you if you're still here?*

I stopped walking and stared at my phone for a second.

Wait, you're here at the game?

Yep. She added a smiley face and a heart emoji after her message.

Still grinning at my phone like an idiot, I wrote back. *Sure, I can take you home. Good thing I've got the spare helmet in the trunk.*

I texted her directions on how to find the players' parking lot, telling her I'd meet her there. She must have already been walking around outside because it didn't take her long to arrive. I caught sight of her before she saw me, which gave me a chance to just stand there and admire her for a moment. Wilder always looked pretty, but she looked especially lovely in her Bay Birds shirt with her blond hair pulled back in a ponytail. It was so cool of her to come to the game and surprise me like this. I wondered if she'd waited to see how my pitching performance went before she told me she was here. If it had gone badly, she might have pretended she hadn't seen the game. Wilder was thoughtful like that.

Brady saw her and waved, making the fans standing near her go crazy. She laughed and talked with some of the kids nearby. Clearly, they were impressed that Wilder knew Brady personally. There was a cute little boy, maybe five or six years old, who seemed really excited to see Brady. Wilder motioned for him to go over, and he cheerfully obliged, blowing the kid's mind.

I'd been so distracted watching Wilder that it took me a moment to realize some of the fans were calling *my* name. That was a first. Usually there was just a lot of smack talk launched my way. This time, some of the fans wanted my autograph. I walked over to the fence and reached up to grab a few baseballs and Bay Bird hats the fans handed me to sign. Out of the corner of my eye, I was pleased to see Wilder had noticed. It was a huge boost to my ego that she'd not only seen me pitch well for once, but that she'd also witnessed the fact that I actually had some fans in Baltimore now.

I signed quickly so as not to keep her waiting. Then I went over to my bike and slid my helmet on.

"Gotta go," Wilder said to the kids near her. "That's my ride."

She gestured toward the gate that the guard opened for me when my motorcycle approached. Once the gate was closed behind me, I hopped off the bike to grab Wilder's helmet from the trunk. The guard was kind enough to run interference, politely but firmly keeping the fans at a safe distance.

As I handed Wilder her helmet, one of the kids asked, "Wow, is Cam Becker your boyfriend?"

She simply laughed and shrugged instead of answering. I couldn't blame her. It was one hell of a loaded question, considering we'd never formally discussed our relationship.

And yet, I was surprised how disappointed I was that she hadn't said yes. I would have been cool with that. More than cool. But how could she know that if I didn't talk to her about it?

We hit the road, and before long we were riding high. Damn, it felt so good to be out on the open road with Wilder's arms wrapped around my waist. Great night at the ballpark and the perfect woman with me to enjoy it. Life didn't get much better than this.

But then it did get even better.

Her roommate wasn't home, and before long, Wilder and I were having sex in her bed. She dug her nails into my back, crying out my name over and over again as I rocked her fucking world.

In New York, she'd dealt with me at my worst. Now she was learning a fun lesson about my mood after a great night at the ballpark. Feeling confident made me horny as hell, and it also made me dominant and in control. I usually gave my best performances in bed after a good performance on the mound.

"Oh ... oh my God ... Cam," Wilder panted as I drilled her hard. Grabbing onto my back for dear life, she threw her head back and thrust her breasts forward. God*damn* she looked hot. I slipped my fingers between her legs and stroked and stroked. Wilder's eyes rolled back in her head like they always did when I gave it to her good. I hoped like hell she was close because I was dangerously close myself.

"Oh ... oh ... C—C—am," she barely managed to say as

her body quaked with orgasmic bliss. Watching and hearing her come sent me over the edge. I came and came *hard* inside her, growling like an animal as I experienced the most mind-blowingly satisfying climax of my life.

We groaned in unison as I climbed off her and collapsed onto the bed beside her.

"Holy hell, that was amazing," Wilder said breathlessly.

I didn't think I'd felt prouder or more confident in my life. Thoroughly pleasuring Wilder seemed an even bigger and better accomplishment than getting the win at the ballpark tonight. Of course, enjoying my own explosive orgasm felt pretty damn good too.

Wilder snuggled up closer to me, filling me with the familiar rush of tenderness I always got after sex with her and only her. Before long, her breathing grew heavier. She had fallen asleep.

I found myself smiling as I lay there in bed. I loved that I'd worn her out with my enthusiastic lovemaking, and I loved that she felt so safe and comfortable in my arms that she could fall asleep.

Then the doubts started to creep in. Sure, I was great to be with when things were going well, but I could be a total ass when things were bad. How long could I expect her to put up with my moodiness when I was in a pitching slump? Sooner or later I was gonna fuck things up. I was just too rough around the edges for a tenderhearted woman like her. With my parents and now my job in Baltimore, I'd managed to royally screw things up by saying the wrong thing at the wrong time. It was only a matter of time before I slipped up with Wilder.

Her recent audition had gone well. Like, really well. I was so happy and relieved when she'd called to tell me. All morning the day of her audition I'd been worried sick. From what she'd told me, she might hear back about the results as early as next week. I wanted nothing more than for her to get the part and for all her dreams to come true.

Even if it meant her traveling all over the country and forgetting all about me.

Maybe that was best for her.

Suddenly, I didn't feel so confident about anything anymore.

20

CAM

Wilder and I met up at Power Bar and Grill for the bar's first karaoke night. Rusty had been trying out some different events to bring in more business on weeknights, including stuff like trivia games, dart contests, and such. This Thursday night happened to be a rare night off for the Bay Birds, so I was able to come out and support my buddy. Not that I was gonna go anywhere near a microphone, but I was happy to sit and drink beer and watch other people make fools of themselves. And of course Wilder wouldn't make a fool of herself. Oh hell no. She could get up there and sing and show everybody how it's done.

While I sat at the bar waiting for Wilder, who was wrapping up a shift at Weaver's Steak House, I watched as a young Bay Birds fan nervously approached Rusty for an autograph. I was glad to see Rusty still got some attention as a former ballplayer. I couldn't imagine how painful it was not to be able to play because of his heart condition. Owning this sports bar was his way of staying connected to baseball and to its loyal fans. Hell, even if people had never heard of Rusty considering he'd only played in the majors for a couple of years, there was a huge photograph of him in a Bay Birds uniform behind the bar. It was hilarious watching people do a double take when they looked at the picture and then saw the same tall redheaded guy tending bar. The funniest part was the inscription on the picture, which read *The Greatest Has-Been in All of Baseball.* Rusty told me the framed photograph had been a gift from his friends on the team when he opened the bar, and I gave him a lot of credit for displaying it so proudly.

Power Bar and Grill was already a fairly popular place in Baltimore, and it was gaining traction all the time. Rusty was really in his element here, and I was happy he'd landed on his feet after damn near dropping dead on the field. I would have thought being surrounded by all things sports and baseball would be depressing for him, but it clearly wasn't. Many times I'd seen him get into animated discussions with baseball fans in the bar.

Rusty talked and laughed with the young Bay Birds fan who looked to be about ten years old. The kiddo no longer seemed nervous—Rusty had put him at ease. The two talked for a little while, then Rusty whispered something to the kid and gestured over at me. Not gonna lie, it felt good when the little boy's eyes lit up. Rusty had tipped him off that there was another Bay Birds player in the house, but it was obvious by the look on the kid's face that he knew exactly who I was. And it was pretty cool. I had to admit, Baltimore had some great baseball fans, loyal and support-ive. I smiled and nodded at the kid, which made his face light up even more. I did my best to make it clear he was welcome to come over for an autograph.

And soon he did.

"Hey there, kiddo," I said as the boy approached me. "Nice Bay Birds shirt."

"Thanks," he said as his eyes opened even wider, like he couldn't believe he was talking to me. One of the major perks of this baseball gig was making a kid's day.

"I just saw you pitch," the boy said excitedly. "I was at the game!"

Nice. So he saw my last appearance on the mound, which was a decent one.

"Cool, I'm glad you were there cheering us on," I told him.

I heard a *clink* as a black Sharpie marker hit my beer glass. I glanced over at Rusty to see him grinning at me and the kid.

Laughing, I said, "I think Rusty Power is telling me you might like an autograph."

"Yeah!" the kid yelled. "I mean, you know, yes please."

I chuckled. This kid's mama had raised him right. Rusty had already signed his white Bay Birds shirt, so I looked for another place to sign.

"Here okay?" I asked, pointing underneath the Bay Birds logo on the front of his shirt.

"Yeah, yeah!"

Careful not to smudge, I signed the shirt for him.

"Thank you, thank you, thank you!" he said before running off to show his parents.

"Making friends, are we?"

I looked up to see Wilder had arrived. She must have been watching me interact with the kid. I'd always heard women were suckers for a man who was good with kids, and the look on her face certainly confirmed that. She smiled sweetly at me, clearly pleased to see how nice I'd been to the kid. And bonus points for me, she knew I hadn't done it just to impress her. I hadn't even realized she was there until she'd spoken up.

"Yup," was all I said.

"Hey, Cam," said the guy next to me at the bar. "I know I'm not exactly a cute little kid, but could I get an autograph too?"

"Fellow Harley man," I said, glancing at his Harley Davidson shirt. "Sure thing."

The guy handed me a napkin and I signed it with the Sharpie.

"Thanks, dude," the Harley guy said, gratefully accepting the napkin. "You been lookin' real good out there lately. Reminded me a lot of Justin Verlander."

"That's high praise indeed. Thanks, man," I said, fist-bumping the guy. I was starting to like Baltimore baseball fans more by the minute. And it was kinda nice not to be universally hated by the city anymore.

During the time I'd been yakking with bar patrons, Wilder had gotten a drink and taken the seat next to me.

"Sorry, sorry. Not trying to ignore you," I said, turning my attention to her, where it belonged.

"No problem." She sipped her beer. "I think it's nice of you to talk shop with Bay Bird fans."

The warm look in her eyes told me she was being sincere. I couldn't help thinking of the way my mom used to flip out whenever my dad wasn't paying total attention to her. Didn't matter if he was talking to another woman, a man, or even a dog. She got super pissed off and would either give him the silent treatment when they got home or she'd start screaming at him. Either way, he was screwed. Sometimes I had to remind myself I didn't need to be on guard like that. Wilder was nothing like my mother.

A woman approached the microphone up on the small stage in the corner of the bar. She introduced herself and explained how the whole karaoke thing worked, and then she encouraged people to come forward and get the party started.

"You heard the lady," I said, nudging Wilder. "Get on up there."

"No way," she said. "I'm just here to watch and cheer people on."

"What?" I asked, feeling genuinely disappointed. Forget random weirdos in the bar, I wanted to hear her sing.

Wilder sighed gently.

"What's the matter?"

She laughed softly. "Okay, how do I say this without sounding conceited? Karaoke is supposed to be fun and silly with no pressure. If I got up there ..." She trailed off, looking uncomfortable.

"Ah, I see. If you got up there, you'd blow the roof off the place and nobody would want to follow you."

"Well, not exactly," Wilder said modestly. "But I am a professional, so it's different for me. It would kinda be like if you did the Speed Pitch booth at the county fair. You'd blow a hole in the wall with your fastball."

"Yeah, he would," said the Harley man next to me, making Wilder laugh.

I noticed Harley Guy checking her out, but at least he did it discreetly. It was pretty clear she was with me, and I didn't think the guy would make a move on her or anything. But he definitely checked out her rack.

Honestly, I couldn't blame him. By now I was getting used to men staring at Wilder everywhere she went. It came with the territory of dating an incredibly beautiful woman. It was a wonder she wasn't stuck-up about it, but she really wasn't. I got the feeling she sometimes got tired of being stared at, but she took it in stride. I thought back to the day I first met her, recalling how she'd hidden out in the back trying to be invisible. Yet I'd found her anyway, poor thing.

Rusty wandered over to us.

"Damn, I hope people will actually do this thing," he said, intently watching the stage. So far, nobody had volunteered to sing.

I looked over at Wilder.

"I will if there's no takers," she said. "But give it a minute. Trust me. All it takes is for one brave person to be the first and then the floodgates will open up. You'll see."

"I hope so," Rusty said.

"Why don't you get on up there and show us how it's done, sailor?" I said to him.

He laughed heartily. "Oh dear God, no. Believe me, *nobody* wants to hear me sing. I'm trying to bring customers in, not drive them away."

Two women in their thirties finally walked up to the stage.

"See, there ya go," Wilder said.

"Whew," Rusty said.

The women performed a silly, giggly version of "I Want It That Way" by the Backstreet Boys. As Wilder had predicted, that broke the ice and soon people were lining up. The next thing we knew, we were treated to fairly terrible renditions of songs like "Wannabe" by the Spice Girls, "Single Ladies" by Beyoncé, and the Queen classic "Bohemian Rhapsody." It turned out to be a lot of fun. With beer flowing freely and Wilder by my side, how could it not be entertaining?

No matter how terrible the performers were, Wilder cheered them on like they were rock stars. I was impressed at the way she seemed happy to let other people shine, even though she was undoubtedly the best singer in the place. When there was finally a lull in the karaoke line, I figured I'd try to coax her up there again.

"Won't you *please* get up there and sing, Wilder? Pretty please? For me?" I asked, batting my eyelashes at her.

Wilder laughed, and I could see I was wearing her down.

"Come on. Everybody else had their shot tonight, so nobody has to follow your Tony-level performance if they don't want to."

"Can your girl sing?" Harley Guy asked. I didn't argue with him when he called Wilder my girl. I kind of loved that.

"Dude, you have *no* idea."

"Well, then get on up there," he said, waving his hand toward the stage.

Wilder hesitated. But she was considering it.

"Yeah, girl," said some random guy at a nearby high-top table. "Do it, do it!"

I didn't like that guy already. I didn't like the way he looked at Wilder. Somehow, it felt different than when Harley Guy looked at her. He kept doing the quick "glance at her tits and store the information for later" that guys often do when they're horny but trying not to be disrespectful to a pretty lady. High-top Table Guy leered at her like she was a piece of meat.

"Do you really think I should go up there?" Wilder asked. "You don't think it's like, you know, showing off?"

"Of course it's showing off, but what's wrong with that? You bust your ass to be a good singer, so why not perform for the nice people? If you do, I promise we'll go to a county fair and I'll win you a bunch of stuffed animals at the Speed Pitch booth."

She laughed happily, her pretty eyes lighting up.

"Okay, fine."

"Yes!" I said, pumping my fist in the air. Except for the occasional car radio singalong, I hadn't heard Wilder really sing since the wedding. Now that I thought about it, I felt kinda bad. I should have asked her to sing for me. After all, she'd seen me pitch several times.

I watched as she conferred with the karaoke lady to decide on a song. I could hardly wait for Wilder to show off those pipes of hers.

High-top Table Guy was still leering at her. He was a big dude, tall and certainly wide, with long dark hair and a stubble of beard. I hated everything about that guy. He just seemed creepy, and I wondered how Wilder dealt with guys like that when I wasn't around. It was a scary thought.

Oh hell yeah, I thought when I heard the first notes of "I Will Always Love You." A great song choice that would showcase Wilder's incredible range and talent. It always cracked me up when people used that song at their weddings. Though it was a bold and powerful song, it wasn't exactly romantic. The lyrics were about a woman who knows the relationship is doomed because she's not right for the guy. As I listened to Wilder's perfect, angelic voice, I couldn't help worrying those lyrics could very well apply to us. I wasn't exactly right for her either. She wanted a Prince Charming. The opposite of me.

I chose to ignore the lyrics for now so I could focus on the sheer pleasure of hearing her voice. The entire bar was enraptured, as I'd known they would be. People stopped to stare. And to listen.

Oh yeah. Wilder was definitely gonna get the part in *Beauty and the Beast.* No one at that audition could possibly have outshone her.

"Look at the tits on her," High-top Table Guy muttered.

I drew in a deep breath, trying to stay calm.

"Why don't you just concentrate on her singing?" I said through clenched teeth.

"Hard to do that when she's got a rockin' bod like that. Got *me* hard, for sure."

The rest of the Neanderthals at his table laughed, which just egged him on.

"Love to get me some of that," he said.

Wilder got to the chorus and really nailed it. People whistled and cheered. I did my best to focus on the friendly, supportive crowd and not the bastards next to me.

"Those legs are long enough to leave heel marks on the roof of my car," the prick said, making his buddies chuckle.

"Show some respect, all right?" I said.

I heard one of his pals mutter something about the singer being my girlfriend. They knew they were getting a rise out of me.

"What the fuck is it to you, choir boy? You some kinda saint? Too good to appreciate a sexy woman? Maybe you're just a faggot."

My nostrils flared. I didn't give a shit about being called gay, but the slur bothered me.

"Watch your mouth. There's kids here."

"*Fuck that,*" he said louder.

Wilder nailed another perfect note, revving the crowd up even more. I tried to focus on her, trying to relish her moment, but it was tough.

"You just know she's a whore in bed. I'd pay top dollar for that."

My muscles tensed.

"Definitely a slut."

I cracked my knuckles.

Wilder finished strong, her powerful voice taking over

the place and making it feel like Madison Square Garden instead of a local Baltimore bar. People went crazy, clapping and applauding and even giving her a standing ovation. Wilder smiled and waved graciously, modestly, but I knew her heart was pumping like crazy, like mine did when I struck out the side.

That's my girl.

"I'm gonna fuck that cunt's brains out."

And that was when my fist connected with that fucker's face with all the force of a ninety-mile-an-hour fastball. Fuck Speed Pitch. I wanted to blow a hole in this guy's skull.

Then I realized I was turning into my father. Sure, my mom screamed a lot, but my dad was the one punching holes in the drywall.

People screamed. Rusty ran over.

"What the hell, Cam?" He watched in horror as the guy I punched staggered to his feet, bleeding pretty good from where I'd busted his cheek open.

Harley Guy came to my defense. "Had it comin,' man. That guy was talking shit about Cam's girl. Really twisted stuff."

Rusty's expression softened. Wilder was like a sister to him. And he knew how much I cared about her.

Wilder rushed over to me, eyes wide in shock.

When I looked into her sweet blue-green eyes, I had zero regrets. Nobody talked like that about Wilder. *Nobody.*

"He was defending your honor," Harley Guy said proudly. "Believe me, that asshole deserved what he got."

"He said ..." I paused, not wanting to repeat anything that jerkoff had said about her. "He was being disrespectful to you."

Wilder nodded wearily. It was clear this wasn't her first

rodeo with this kind of creep. Well, it wasn't gonna happen anymore. Not on my watch.

Bloody High-top Table Guy grinned menacingly at me. "I'm gonna sue you for assault. Bay Bird's owner will love that. Your career is over, man."

The truth hit me like a ton of bricks.

He was right. Gary Devilbuss ran a tight ship. He didn't tolerate any bad behavior from his players.

Wilder covered her mouth with her hand, and her eyes filled with fear. I still wasn't sorry I'd decked the guy. She'd been up there singing her heart out, showing just how hard she'd worked all these years to be the best performer she could be. And that sicko kept leering at her, talking about her tits and calling her a cunt.

He called her a cunt.

My fist cocked again just thinking about it. I had to get a fucking grip. I was in enough trouble as it was.

"I'd be glad to call the cops for you," Rusty said to the guy. I had barely registered his words of betrayal before he added, "But I'm afraid I can't be much help because I didn't see what happened. Anybody else see what happened?"

Rusty shot a knowing look at the crowd that had gathered.

"Nope," Harley Guy said. "Didn't see a thing. I was too busy listening to the girl's pretty voice."

He winked at Wilder as he spoke.

"I didn't see anything either," said some other dude nearby.

I looked around and saw nothing but shaking heads. I'd obviously generated a lot of goodwill here among Bay Bird fans during the course of the evening. It helped that the people sitting nearby had heard the guy's sick comments about Wilder.

"I saw what happened," said a woman in her sixties or so who stepped forward.

Shit.

The entire bar fell silent. Now I was really fucked.

Gesturing at High-top Table Guy, she said, "That guy hit you first."

I heard chuckles from around the room. I let out a breath of relief.

"Fuck this," the creepy bastard said. Knowing he'd been beat, he stormed out of the bar, kicking over his chair violently in the process.

"It's okay," Rusty called after him. "Your beer's on the house."

More chuckles from the bar patrons. Harley Guy clapped me on the back before heading back to his seat. The karaoke music started up again.

"I'm sorry, man," I said to Rusty.

"It's okay. I get it. You do what you gotta do sometimes."

I turned to Wilder, who still looked pretty shaken up.

"Cam, is your hand okay?" she asked, her eyes filled with concern.

"Yeah, yeah. It's fine. I'm fine."

My right hand throbbed a bit, but no harm done. Good thing I wasn't pitching tomorrow.

"You sounded incredible up there, Wilder. Hope I didn't ruin it for you."

"You didn't. I'm just glad you're okay," she said, taking my hand in hers, inspecting it for damage.

"I'm okay. I promise."

Wilder nodded, but still seemed a bit upset. She must have thought I was some kind of barbarian, getting into a bar fight like that.

I kept thinking about the lyrics to "I Will Always Love

You." Especially the part that said "*I'm not what you dream of.*" She deserved so much better than me.

A Disney prince never would have punched a guy out like that.

Yep. I knew I'd find a way to fuck things up with Wilder.

21

———————

WILDER

He was defending your honor.

I lay on my couch the next day just daydreaming about Cam. I normally didn't condone violence, but Cam punching that guy was the most romantic thing anyone had ever done for me. I'd never seen him so angry before, and I wondered what the guy had said to get him so riled up. Something disgusting about my body no doubt, but probably nothing I hadn't heard before. Cam had looked so damned sexy when he was angry, but when he saw me, he gazed at me with such tenderness. So unbelievably *dreamy.* He wasn't much for talking about his feelings, so I had to rely on his actions and expressions to figure out what might be going on inside his head. And his heart.

We still hadn't talked about where this relationship was going, which was a bit unnerving. For all I knew, he was still sleeping with other women when he was out on the road with the team. I doubted he was, but I worried about it. Since we'd never said we were official or exclusive, he had the right to do what he wanted. I just wished with all my heart that what he wanted was a commitment. I was so happy being with him, I didn't want to rock the boat by forcing the issue, and yet I couldn't live in limbo like this forever. He had the right to play the field if he wanted to, so to speak. So did I, but that wasn't what I wanted.

What I wanted was to marry Cam Becker and live happily ever after. But that wasn't likely to happen.

I should just ask him what his intentions were, but the answer terrified me. If he said he wanted to keep things casual—and non-exclusive—then we had a problem. I didn't want to be with a man who wasn't all-in. But I didn't want to leave him either. From the get-go, Cam had said he wasn't looking for anything serious. If he had somehow changed his mind about that, wouldn't he have said so by now?

Rather than dwell on the negative, I closed my eyes and went back to reliving last night's events when Cam had dashingly come to my rescue.

My phone buzzed, irritatingly snapping me out of my reverie. If it was anyone other than Cam, I was gonna be super annoyed.

It wasn't Cam.

It was an email with the results of my audition.

Jumping up from the couch, I cried out, "Oh my God, oh my God, oh my God ..."

Fortunately, Kerry was away visiting her parents for a few days. I really needed to be alone when I got the results. The whole thing would be too stressful with an audience.

Please oh please let me have the lead role. My dream role. I was born to play it. Please please please ...

My hands shaking, I clicked on the email.

Then I read and re-read and re-read the message to make sure I was seeing what I thought I was seeing.

Nothing.

I'd gotten nothing.

Forget the lead, I hadn't even landed the part of a townsperson in the damned show. I wouldn't be touring all over the country after all. I was going nowhere. Except to my job at Weaver's, where I'd probably be for the rest of my natural life.

I was completely numb. In shock. When it wore off, I found myself sitting on the couch, sobbing. Just full out, openly weeping. Rather than a release, crying like that made it worse. It made me feel like a loser who couldn't handle rejection.

I'd been turned down for lots of roles over the years, but this one hit different. This was *The One.* Somehow, deep in my bones, I'd really, truly believed that this would be my big break. I had felt so deeply that I would get this part, and I couldn't fathom how badly I'd misjudged the situation. How utterly stupid and naive I'd been. Now I had the results, I didn't understand why on earth I'd thought there was a chance I'd get the lead role in a national production.

I couldn't remember the last time I cried over not getting a part. When I first started out, I used to get upset and discouraged when I got turned down for a role, but over the years I'd toughened up. Or so I'd thought. Ever since my audition for *Beauty and the Beast,* or maybe even since I'd found out about the audition, I'd been daydreaming about traveling the country, performing in major cities in the role of Belle. I'd fantasized about calling my family to give them the big news. Telling them about this huge part I'd won. It had all felt so real, so possible. I'd been mentally and emotionally preparing for it, thinking about how I would give my notice at Weaver's and how I would gather my family all together, humble when I was inwardly screaming *In your face, all you people who told me my dream was stupid.*

Thank God in heaven I hadn't told anyone in my family about the audition. Only the close people in my inner circle of friends knew about it, so that would at least minimize the humiliation when I had to tell them I totally bombed out.

Just thinking about it brought on a fresh bout of tears. My God, I was spiraling out of control. I hated this feeling. Hated feeling like a failure, a pathetic loser. Normally I wasn't so hard on myself, but this rejection hurt so damn much. For the first time in a long time, I didn't know how to deal with the pain.

I thought about Cam. If nothing else, at least I wouldn't have to leave him to do the show. That brought me little comfort, though. I still had no real claim on him. We weren't officially boyfriend and girlfriend. We were ... I didn't know what we were. My relationship with him seemed as uncertain as my career right now. Everything was up in the air, and I felt like I had nothing to cling to. Maybe I should just ask Cam point blank the all-important question about our relationship.

No. That was a *bad* idea. I was not in a good place right now, and the last thing I needed was to ask a question I might not want the answer to. I continued to spiral, feeling worse and worse about myself. Why would he want to be with someone who fell to pieces every time something went wrong? He'd have to deal with my mood swings every time I didn't get a part, which wouldn't be fun for him. Maybe he'd rather be with a bunch of one-night stand types so he didn't have to stick around for the bad times. As usual, I worried that sooner or later Cam was gonna get bored with me. It would have been one thing if I'd actually gotten the part. Sure, we would have had to try to make a long-distance relationship work, but at least Cam would be dating a successful actress. Instead, he was dating a bartender at a steak joint. It simply did not matter how beautiful I was. Pretty got old after a while.

Just ask Danny.

Thinking about that jerk pushed me even further into my depression and anguish. He had rejected me. The *Beauty and the Beast* show had rejected me. I was starting to wonder if my family was right when they told me that pursuing a career in musical theater was a waste of time because it was never gonna happen.

Somebody knocked at the door. I sighed heavily. I didn't have the energy to deal with anyone right now. I thought about simply ignoring whoever it was, but for all I knew, Kerry's plans had changed and she'd forgotten her key or something. Wearily, I heaved myself from the couch and staggered to the door. I *never* opened the door without looking through the peephole first, but I was tired and not thinking straight, so I just opened the door without checking to see who it was.

Cam's eyes flew open wide in horror when he saw my ghastly appearance. I blinked a couple of times, trying to remember what day and time it was. Damn, I really was a mess. Finally, I remembered it was Friday and Cam and I were supposed to go out at around 7pm, since his day game should have been over by then. Apparently, my pity party had caused me to lose track of time.

"Wilder, what the hell happened to you?" he asked, reaching to touch my face. He seemed genuinely frightened, like he thought I might have been assaulted or something.

"I'm okay, Cam," I said, sounding as tired as I was.

His expression relaxed slightly. Then a look of understanding crossed his face.

"You didn't get the part," he said quietly.

I stared at him, overwhelmed that he knew me so well.

Cam understood that not getting my dream role was the one thing in the world that would affect me like this.

"No. I didn't."

God it hurt like hell having to admit it out loud.

Wordlessly, he took my hand and led me over to the couch. Once we were seated, he wrapped his arm around me, and I rested my head on his shoulder. It was safe to literally cry on his shoulder, but I was all cried out.

We sat on the couch for a little while, not saying anything. Just having Cam near me was soothing. After a while, I broke the silence.

"I swear I don't usually act like this when I don't get a part. I never fall apart like this."

"I believe it," Cam said. "This one hit different. This was supposed to be the big one."

My eyes filled with tears all over again. It helped so much that he understood.

"Exactly." I sat up on the couch to face him. Cam looked into my eyes and waited, giving me time to gather my thoughts. It was exactly what I needed. I loved that he didn't offer me well-meaning yet pointless words like *you'll get 'em next time* and *this is just one audition*. I needed to grieve this loss, and he seemed to get it.

"This is gonna so sound over-the-top and melodramatic," I began.

"Say it anyway," he said firmly.

I drew in a deep breath and said, "My heart is broken, and my artist soul is tired."

Cam listened intently. He nodded.

Sighing deeply, I added, "They always say it's not how many times you get knocked down, it's how many times you get back up again. But what they don't tell you is how much harder it gets every time you get kicked in the face. It's not easy to get up when you feel bruised and bloodied."

Cam contemplated my words for a moment. "That's how I felt when I got traded to Baltimore."

He rarely opened up to me about his feelings, and I knew his confession was difficult. I also knew it meant he truly understood what I was going through on a level nobody else in my life ever did. It was hard for people who didn't have the deep-seated need to pursue their dream to understand why we went through all the suffering. They saw us fail time and time again, and they couldn't understand what made us keep going in spite of all the pain and anguish and the terrible odds of making it. I guess it wasn't something you could put into words. With Cam, I didn't have to explain. He simply knew.

He tenderly stroked my face and said, "I would give anything in the world if I could take this pain away from you."

"Thank you," I whispered.

Cam pulled me into his arms and held me for a while. The deep, aching sadness inside me didn't go away, but it eased as he comforted me.

It occurred to me that being with Cam was like being onstage in a way. Sometimes I would stress out and worry about how it would go, but then the time came and it was wonderful. In this beautiful moment, as Cam held me, I stopped worrying he would get bored with me.

He seemed happy with me just the way I was, scars and all.

~

THE NEXT NIGHT, my shift at Weaver's felt like it was never going to end. I hadn't realized how much time I'd spent daydreaming about the *Beauty and the Beast* show. For months now, I'd been mentally and emotionally halfway out the door, thinking this was just a temporary job until my real life began.

Now all that was gone.

The drudgery of the job really got to me tonight. I'd long ago gotten used to giving up my Saturday nights to work, since naturally it was the busiest night of the week at a restaurant and bar. At least dating Cam—or *whatever* I was doing with Cam—made it easier to work weekends since it wasn't like he was available most Friday and Saturday nights. Until now, I also hadn't realized how much of my good mood at work was based on daydreaming about starring in the show. A good chunk of my income came from tips, and I had to be cheerful no matter how I was feeling. Now, that made the job so much harder. All I wanted was to be alone and wallow in self-pity. Instead I was surrounded by the Saturday night bar crowd.

Fortunately, we didn't have any jerky customers tonight, because I really didn't know how well I would have dealt with them. My emotions were raw, and it wouldn't take much for me to snap. Still, the night dragged on and on. Not having the *Beauty and the Beast* show to fantasize about just gave me more time to worry about other things.

I'd been such a hot mess last night, and Cam was incredibly kind and patient with me. Though my freaking out didn't seem to faze him, I couldn't help worrying I'd eventually scare him off with my hysterics. As grateful as I was that he'd been there to comfort me, I hated that he'd had to see me like that. He hadn't known me long enough to know how rare that kind of meltdown was for me. Good Lord, if I flipped out that way every time I didn't get a part, I'd have an ulcer by now. This business was not for the faint of heart, and I prided myself on taking the hits in stride. Even I had my breaking point, and poor Cam had been forced to be there to pick up the pieces.

"Hel-LO!"

A man in his fifties sitting at the bar was snapping his fingers at me. So much for no jerky customers tonight. To be fair, I had no idea how long he'd been trying to get my attention.

"I'm sorry, sir. What can I get for you?"

"A better server," he said, making his buddy next to him laugh.

This isn't your real job. It was my automatic go-to mental response, an instant defense mechanism when somebody treated me like a lowly servant.

But the thought hit different tonight. Maybe this was my real job.

My eyes filled with tears, and I hated like hell that I was letting some asshole get the best of me. I couldn't help it. They say the more you care about something, the more you grieve when you lose it. And dear God, did I care about my singing. It was the heart and soul of who I was.

Numbly, I took the jerkoff's drink order and managed to hand it to him with a smile, even though I still had tears in my eyes. To his credit, the guy looked surprised and even slightly ashamed to see how upset I was. That tiny glimpse of humanity helped a little.

I held it together for the rest of the seemingly endless night. I cried a little in the car on the way home, way too tired for a good, hard sob fest. It wasn't just the exhaustion, though. The pain was already starting to lessen a little. I'd never forget the heartache of this particularly stinging failure, but I also knew there would be other auditions, other parts, other opportunities. For all I knew, an even better opportunity was right around the corner.

I had the day off tomorrow, and I knew exactly what I needed to do to feel better. Singing my heart out, loud and clear, was always incredibly healing for me. Even in the depths of despair, it reminded me of who I was and why I put myself through all this agony. It was never really about being a star and proving everybody wrong. It was about the art, and I needed to reconnect to that part. I'd head to the theater space at the University of Towson tomorrow and release all my pent-up emotions. Even being up on stage without an audience was incredibly cathartic, just what my artistic soul needed.

I was concerned I'd scared Cam off with my craziness, but it wasn't something I could afford to worry about. As insecure as I was about holding on to a man, I deserved a guy who could handle me at my worst. Better to be alone than with a man who didn't support me. Cam had been nothing *but* supportive so far, but I guess I was waiting for the other shoe to drop. It always did.

I stopped to get my mail from the locked metal box in front of my building. I was surprised to see a package had arrived. It was from Cam.

My first thought was that he'd bought me a present to soften the blow of breaking up with me.

Holy crap, where did that thought come from?

Cam had given me no indication whatsoever that he planned to bail out on me, but my vulnerability made me fear the worst. That, land sometimes I forgot how badly Danny's betrayal had messed me up.

I hurried inside so I could rip open the package. Well,

not rip it open. It was marked "Fragile." I sat on the couch and carefully opened the box.

Cam had sent me a beautifully delicate Cinderella music box. It was a ceramic, hand-painted figurine of Cinderella still dressed in rags and holding a bird. I twisted the bottom to wind it up, and it played "A Dream is a Wish Your Heart Makes."

The package included a handwritten note from Cam: *There were plenty of times I never thought it would happen for me either. Then one day I got the call. "You got called up. You're going to the majors, kid." You're gonna make it to the majors, Wilder. I know it. Don't give up.*

Pressing the note against my heart, a deep sense of calm swept over me. I knew, really *knew*, that everything was gonna be okay, no matter what happened. As long as there were good and kind people in the world who cared, every-thing was gonna be all right.

A dream is a wish your heart makes.

Cam could not possibly have picked a more perfect gift for me. I played the song over and over on the gorgeous music box, marveling at how thoughtful he had been to send it. He might be a man of few words, but there was more going on in his head and his heart than I realized some-times. But I still needed answers about our relationship; I couldn't live with this uncertainty forever.

For now, this was more than enough.

I ALREADY FELT a sense of renewed energy the next day as I headed out to the University of Towson. I'd never let profes-sional disappointments get me down for long, and this time should be no different. I knew that once I cued up my music and hit that stage, all the reasons I wanted to be a performer would come flooding back.

The receptionist in the Theater Arts building gave me a sympathetic smile when she checked my ID. I must have still looked pretty depressed, but that was what I was here to fix. I jogged down the hall and punched the key code into the door for the auditorium, hoping like hell I would have the place to myself. I never knew if there was a rehearsal going on or if another college alum was here with the same idea as me. Thankfully, the theater was empty.

There was no question in my mind what song I would sing. "This is Me" from *The Greatest Showman.* It was the perfect selection for my purposes. A powerful song about picking up your broken pieces, soldiering on, and loving yourself just as you were. The song was gorgeous, strong, and courageous, and it was impossible not to feel the same way when I sang it.

The music began, and so did my healing.

Standing in the middle of the stage, I sang the beginning, which was small and quiet. The opening described how it felt to have the sharpest words cut you down. I felt it in my *soul.* Then the song built to a crescendo, sending a flood to drown out those words. I felt that, too. I was doing exactly that.

I sang the ever-loving *hell* out of the song. It didn't matter that nobody was listening. Someday they would. Someday a crowd would experience the love and light I sent out from the stage and shared with the world. Just like the song said: "*Look out. Here I come.*"

Oh hell yeah.

I gave that performance everything I had. As far as I was concerned, singing this song here and now held every bit as much importance as the audition had.

Onstage was where I belonged. It didn't matter if those *Beauty and the Beast* people didn't know it. I *knew* it.

I ended the showstopper of a song with a tremendous flourish, and this time the tears in my eyes were of triumph, endurance, and belief in myself.

This. Is. Me.

Breathing heavily and reveling in the sheer joy of performing and just being alive, I glanced to the back of the theater to find I wasn't alone after all.

Cam was here.

22

CAM

I stared at Wilder, utterly enthralled. She was incredible each and every time I had the privilege to see her perform, but this stage appearance was on a whole other level. I wasn't familiar with the song, but I could tell it was like an anthem for her. Something that gave her the power and strength to keep going. The lyrics were inspiring, and no doubt exactly what she needed to bolster her spirits.

She caught sight of me when she finished singing, and I hoped I hadn't intruded on a private moment. I'd spent the whole morning puttering around my apartment worrying about her. Even though I understood exactly what she was going through, I had no clue what to do or what to say to make it better. I'd done the best I could that night to comfort her, but like always, I knew I wasn't enough. I was terrible at expressing my feelings and was constantly at a loss for words.

I'd called her and texted her earlier today, but she hadn't responded. I started to get worried before it finally dawned on me where she was. Lucky for me, the first college kid I ran into on campus was a huge Bay Birds fan and was more than happy to give me directions to the theater building.

Wilder looked dazed when she saw me in the back of the room. I made the slow walk toward her, hoping she didn't mind my presence. I climbed the theater steps to join her onstage.

"Cam, what in the world are you doing here? How did you find me?"

Shrugging, I said, "I remembered what you told me when we were in New York about how your old college lets you use the theater space. I figured now more than ever, you needed to sing."

"Wow," Wilder said softly.

She certainly wasn't upset that I was here.

Cool.

My heart caught in my throat as I stood there for a moment, overwhelmed by her. Everything about her. Her beauty was only the beginning. I was awed by her talent, her strength, her resilience. Her kindness. Everything about her was wonderful. Everything, everything, everything.

For the rest of my life, whatever happened with us, I would always remember that this was the moment I realized I was in love with Wilder.

"You okay?" she asked, looking concerned after a period of silence that was lengthy, even for me.

"Oh y—yeah. Yeah," I stuttered. Smooth, real smooth.

I scanned the stage she'd just set on fire with her passionate performance. Then I turned back to her.

"Wilder ... how could you think for one moment that you're not gonna make it someday?"

Her beautiful eyes filled with tears, and she put her hand over her heart.

"That was amazing, Wilder. Like really, truly amazing.

I've never seen anything like it," I told her, meaning every syllable. "And you know I don't even like showtunes." I didn't know why the hell I'd thought it was a good idea to add that last part.

Wilder burst out laughing. "That's a good point."

At least she found my comment funny and not offensive.

"Cam," she said as she tenderly ran her fingers through my hair. "I loved the music box."

I'd already forgotten about the gift I sent her. I guess I wasn't completely terrible at this kind of thing.

"It was lovely and so perfect," she said softly.

"I know *Beauty and the Beast* is your favorite and not *Cinderella,* but I figured, you know ... maybe pump the brakes on the *Beauty and the Beast* stuff for the moment."

She laughed again. "Yes, exactly. That's what made it so perfect. Thank you."

"You're welcome." I almost added "sweetheart." I was fucking in love with this woman, and yet I couldn't even call her sweetheart. I'd bet hundreds of guys would kill to have Wilder as their girlfriend, and they'd have no problem sweeping her off her feet and giving her the fairy tale she deserved. She adored all things Disney, and I couldn't help thinking of her as the princess and me as the troll living under the bridge.

Despite my usual fumbling, this was a sweet moment, and I didn't want it to end. So, as usual, I let my actions speak louder than my words.

I dipped my head and kissed Wilder, and she melted in my arms. At least I was fairly confident I was a good kisser. Her soft moans seemed to confirm it. She wrapped her arms around me, and we kissed for a while. I hoped nobody would come in and find us using the stage for naughty, non-theater-related purposes. The last thing she needed right now was to have her stage privileges revoked.

As our kissing grew hotter and heavier, I thought about asking her if she wanted to go back to my place. I had plenty of time before tonight's game.

But then I remembered I'd barged in on her private time. Maybe she wanted to stay and sing some more.

"I should probably go," I said, reluctantly pulling away from her.

"Why?" Wilder asked, looking shocked and a little sad.

"I'm not saying I want to. What I *want* to do is ravish you right here and now on the stage."

She laughed softly, looking relieved.

"But I don't want to intrude any more than I have already. This is your time, your thing."

"It's okay. I'm done for now. Really. I'm liking this 'ravishing' idea of yours."

"Really?" I asked as my eyes flew open wide.

She laughed again. "Yes, but not here. I'd still like to be able to use this space in the future, you know. Pretty sure onstage sex is frowned upon."

"Fair enough. Your place or mine?" I asked.

"Yours."

"Cool."

We walked down from the stage together, and she turned off the lights on our way out.

"I really didn't show up here trying to hit you up for sex, you know."

Wilder giggled and rested her head on my shoulder as we headed out.

"I know, Cam. I know."

We went back to my apartment and spent a blissful afternoon in my bed. I wanted to do absolutely anything I could to comfort Wilder. Seeing her face when I'd first gotten to her place had been quite a shock. I didn't want to see that agonized expression ever again. I could tell she'd been crying. Like, hardcore sobbing before I'd arrived. Her eyes and face had been swollen. Seeing her like that had been a gut-punch straight to my heart.

I might never know the right things to say, but I sure as hell knew what to do to make my girl feel good. We had sex twice, with a short nap in between sessions. Kind of like an intermission, to put it in theater terms. For Act One, I took my time with Wilder. I went down on her, stroking her clit, hoping to get her totally focused on sex and pleasure and not on her career woes. Judging by her sensual moans and the way she grabbed the sheets tightly in her fists, it worked. I pleasured her for as long as I could, and by the end she was begging for release.

Good thing we were doing it at my place and not hers with her roommate around. Wilder was always pretty noisy during sex, but I'd never heard her scream that loud before. I gave her a moment to start breathing normally again after her climax, then I took her from behind. We moved together in perfect rhythm, and it wasn't long before I was calling out *her* name.

As always, I started second-guessing myself again. A Disney prince wouldn't fuck a woman from behind like that. He'd be tender and gentle, *making love* to her rather than having wild sex. And yet I didn't hear any complaints from Wilder. Besides, a Disney prince might be tender and romantic, but it was hard to imagine him actually getting a woman off.

Holy fuck, I was lying next to a gorgeous, naked woman and thinking about cartoon characters having sex.

"Oh, Cam," Wilder moaned as she cuddled closer to me.

Hell yeah. No complaints here. Take that, Prince Charming.

After we rested, we did it again, and it kinda was more romantic the second time around. Our sexual need wasn't as desperate, so we were able to take it slow and enjoy each other. Act Two was more traditional, with me on top. Sex with Wilder felt different since I realized I was in love with her. I might be terrible about expressing my emotions, but I still felt things deeply. My love for Wilder certainly was deep.

Maybe in about ten years I'd finally get the balls to tell her. If she wasn't long gone by then.

"Don't you have a game tonight?" she asked after recovering from her second orgasm of the day. Seriously, was there anything hotter than a pretty girl in your bed after you'd rocked her fucking world? She looked so sleepy, so thoroughly satisfied. My pride surged just looking at her. Words often failed, but my cock never did.

"Yeah, I do." I kissed her and reluctantly got out of bed.

Wilder smiled, eyeing my naked body up and down. "I'm liking this view."

I chuckled. "I'm glad you do. Hey, did you want to go to the game tonight? I'm pitching."

"I'd love to, Cam. But I've got rehearsal."

"Oh right. I forgot."

"Speaking of which, the show opens pretty soon. I know you hate musicals, but do you want to go?"

"Are you in it?"

Wilder looked confused. "Well, yeah."

"Then I wanna go. Anything you're in, I wanna see."

"Thanks, Cam," she said with a sweet smile.

After I got dressed, I went over and kissed her again, still naked in bed.

"You can hang out here as long as you want. Just lock up when you leave."

"Will do," she said.

I gazed at her for a moment.

I love you.

The words were *right there,* but somehow, I just couldn't say them.

"Good luck out there tonight," she said.

"Thanks. Good lu— I mean, break a leg at rehearsal."

She laughed softly. "Thanks."

Break a leg. Sure, *those* three words I could say.

23

———

CAM

The next week I went to see Wilder's musical at the community theater. I was excited to finally get the chance to watch her perform in an actual show. I sat in the audience on a Saturday afternoon doing my best to keep a low profile. Not that I minded being recognized by Bay Birds fans, but this was Wilder's thing, and I didn't want to steal her thunder.

I flipped through the show's program and smiled to see the name Wilder Price. I was already so proud of her. She was playing some character named Johanna. She'd reminded me before the show that she wasn't playing a major part. With sadness in her eyes, she'd said she had wanted to keep her mind clear for her big audition. I told her I couldn't wait to see her onstage, no matter how small her part might be.

As much as I'd wanted to come to opening night last night, I had to settle for a Saturday matinee because of my baseball schedule. I looked up at the stage, eager for the show to start. When I saw that in addition to the American flag off to the side of the stage, they also had the Maryland flag, I shook my head. What *was* it with Marylanders and that damned flag? I'd wager most people in other states didn't even know what their state flag looked like. Just for fun, I glanced around to see how many glimpses of that black, yellow, red, and white flag I could find. I saw five shirts with some version of it. One lady had a Maryland flag purse. Another had a pretty cool shirt that featured both the Maryland flag and the Bay Birds logo.

I stopped counting weirdos with flags when the lights dimmed.

The show was surprisingly badass. I wasn't at all familiar with the story, but *Sweeney Todd* turned out to be about this creepy, murderous barber who was hell-bent on revenge.

Cool.

Sometimes I forgot that not all musicals were fluffy, gooey romances with princesses in ball gowns. *The Phantom of the Opera* had its moments, and the show we saw in New York about the dead ex-wives of Henry the VIII wasn't bad at all.

I couldn't help noticing the guy who played Sweeney Todd was fairly good-looking. Sure, they put makeup and shit on him to make him look older and grungier, but it was obvious he was hot underneath. I was relieved that Wilder's character was his daughter, so I didn't have to worry about any onstage make-out sessions.

It was a shame Wilder had turned down the lead role of Mrs. Lovett, Sweeney's creepy and hilarious sidekick. She would have nailed the part. I hoped she wasn't too upset that she'd given it up in favor of an audition for people who were too stupid to know talent if it punched them dead in the face.

Not that I was bitter or anything.

I would never forget the look on Wilder's face that day

she found out she didn't get her dream role. I wanted to kick the ass of anyone who had anything to do with the decision not to cast her.

Guilt crept in when my mind started to wander during the show. Until Wilder showed up. My heart rate sped up the moment I laid eyes on her. That woman was stunningly beautiful. She was always pretty, but onstage in her element and doing what she was born to do, she positively glowed. And she sang like an angel. According to the program, the first song she performed was called "Green Finch and Linnet Bird." It was in a higher register than the songs she normally sang, and once again I was blown away by her incredible range.

Everyone's eyes were on her. Of course, that was how it should be. And yet it made me uncomfortable for some reason. Sure, men stared at her everywhere we went, and she just ignored them. But it was oddly unsettling to think she could have any man in this room if she wanted.

Great, so it turned out the hot young sailor who'd been hanging with Sweeney this whole time was Wilder's—I mean Johanna's—love interest. Damn. I'd forgotten about that Anthony character from earlier in the show. Guess I should have seen that coming.

Ugh. So Anthony wanted to marry Johanna and he was all heroic and rescued her and all that crap. Maybe I was wrong about Wilder being better off playing Mrs. Lovett. The character of Johanna seemed perfect for my sweet Disney princess.

Well, she wasn't technically *mine*.

And it was my fault that she wasn't. After all, I'd never asked her to be my girlfriend. As much as I wished to make her mine, I wanted to do what was best for her. The odds were pretty good that I was *not* best for her.

The more I watched her onstage with the Anthony guy, the more uncomfortable I felt. The guy playing him, some dude named Zeke Anderson according to the program, was the living embodiment of everything I was not. Dreamy and romantic, openly professing his love for her.

As much as I loved Wilder, I couldn't ever picture myself being that kind of guy. Never the one with all the right, sweet, romantic words. No. I said stuff like *"You fucking got this. Give 'em hell, Belle."*

I cringed just thinking about it. I didn't know what the right words of encouragement were, but I know those weren't them. No doubt Zeke would know what to say to encourage Wilder. He had probably said all the right things to her before her audition. They were scene partners after all. They must have talked about it. For all I knew, he'd called her the day of the audition when all I'd done was send a lousy text. And I bet a sensitive theater type guy like Zeke wouldn't have punched a guy in a bar like I had.

Wait a minute—sensitive theater guy … Was it too much to hope Zeke was gay?

In my mind he was, and that thought helped me relax a little and enjoy the rest of the show. The finale was surprisingly bloody and violent. Pretty wicked for a musical.

The actors came out to mingle with the crowd afterward, and I scanned the place looking for Wilder. I caught sight of Sweeney first, and I noted that he was indeed even more attractive with his makeup scrubbed off. I shook his hand and congratulated him on his performance.

"Thanks, man. I appreciate that," he said warmly. Nice guy. I hoped he didn't have the hots for Wilder.

I needed to get a grip already. I'd never considered myself the jealous type, but then again, I'd never been in love before.

My adrenaline surged when I finally spotted Wilder walking toward me. She was stunning, still in her costume and shimmering with a performer's high. She took my breath away.

Unfortunately, that Zeke guy was walking with her. Great. Now I'd have to play nice with the guy who'd been wooing Wilder onstage all night.

"Well, what did you think?" Wilder asked breathlessly.

"Sweetheart, you were amazing," I told her, pulling her into my arms for a hug. Apparently, I needed the threat of another man to finally call her that.

"Thanks," she said as I held her for a moment. I breathed her sweet scent before reluctantly releasing her.

"You were great, too," I said to Zeke, extending my hand.

"What, no hug?" he joked before shaking my hand.

He *definitely* might be gay.

"Thanks for coming," he said with a friendly smile, making it hard to hate him. Wilder seemed at ease around him, which meant he must be treating her well. Good thing. I'd hate to have to punch him out too for disrespecting her. "Oh, I gotta run. I see my mom. Nice meeting you, Cam. Catch you later, Wilder!"

He knew my name. Either he was a Bay Birds fan or, better yet, Wilder had told him all about me.

"So what's his deal?" I asked before I could stop myself. "He gay?"

"What?" Wilder asked. Then she shook her head. "No, he is not gay. That's such a theater stereotype. Shame on you, Cam."

"Yeah, I know. Sorry," I mumbled.

She paused for a moment. "Well, okay. Our Sweeney Todd is gay. But that doesn't mean anything," she said, giggling and punching me lightly in the shoulder.

"But you're sure Zeke's not gay?"

"Trust me. I know for *sure* he's not gay."

Her statement put a horrible image of Zeke having sex with her in my head, and it must have showed on my face.

"No, no. We never hooked up or anything," she added quickly. I was ashamed that she could tell how jealous I was.

"He just, you know, asked me out once. I said no."

"Why?" I couldn't help asking. The guy seemed perfect for her.

"I was ... seeing someone at the time." She looked uncomfortable.

"Me?"

Wilder blushed slightly. "Well, yeah."

"Oh," I said with a nod.

Clearly she was as uncertain about our relationship as I was. And yet I was pretty sure she hadn't been with anyone else since we'd started dating or doing whatever we were doing. I couldn't even imagine being with another woman either, and I knew damn well I should tell her.

But right now I was questioning absolutely everything. The only thing I knew for sure was that I loved Wilder. Totally, crazily, and helplessly. But what if I was holding her back from meeting the man of her dreams?

Wilder deserved so much better than a guy like me.

So maybe the time had come for me to step aside so she could get on with her quest to find the guy she was supposed to be with.

The mere thought of letting her go made me sick to my stomach. But the thought of convincing her to settle for me instead of the dreamy, romantic hero she deserved made me feel even worse.

"You okay?" she asked, her eyes filled with concern.

"Yeah, of course. Wilder, you were so incredible up

there. I'm so proud of you. I didn't even know you could sing that high."

She laughed. "Some of those notes are tough to reach, but I can usually manage."

"You did more than manage. You sang the shit out of it."

Wilder laughed again and threw her arms around me, her eyes sparkling.

Though I guess she didn't mind what I'd said, inside I was cringing again.

Sang the shit out of it.

Not exactly Shakespeare, was it?

Ugh.

MY MIND SPUN as I drove to the ballpark after Wilder's show. More than anything, I could have used the wind therapy, out on the open road on my Harley, but thunderstorms were threatening in the area, so I'd been forced to take the car. I kept imagining Wilder with Zeke, and every scenario my brain came up with showed them as the perfect couple. It was all too easy to picture them hanging out at rehearsals, running over their lines.

Why hadn't I ever run lines with Wilder?

I knew the answer. First of all, she'd never asked me. Second, she probably knew I would be terrible at it. Awkward and uncomfortable. I couldn't express my own emotions, let alone somebody else's on the page.

Unfortunately, I didn't have to imagine Zeke and Wilder kissing because I'd seen it onstage this afternoon. They certainly seemed to have a lot of chemistry up there. He was such a handsome guy. To be fair, so was I. But that wasn't enough. The two of them must have so much in common.

He probably liked Disney stuff too. Hell, there were so many musicals out there based on Disney films, he'd probably played a prince in some of them already.

Sighing heavily, I flipped on the car radio, though it wouldn't have the same healing effect as blasting rock music on my bike. Then I got an idea.

I had one of those paid radio subscriptions with hundreds of channels, so once I got to a stoplight, I scanned the stations until I found the Disney one. I really hadn't given Disney music a chance. I didn't have any nieces or nephews, and I didn't have kids. I'd never had the occasion to watch any of those movies. The music could be great for all I knew.

I made it through about three songs in before I snapped.

"I can't do it! I can't take it!" I quickly flipped to my favorite alternative rock station.

Banging my hands on the steering wheel, I admitted defeat. There was no getting around it. I could not bear listening to Disney tunes, and I still wasn't a fan of musicals. No matter how much I loved Wilder, I'd never learn to like that shit.

But I loved that Wilder was into it. Her love of all things Disney was incredibly endearing, and her passion for singing and musicals was sexy as hell. Being with a woman who got excited over stuff like that was fun. It made me smile to watch her light up when she looked at the *Beauty and the Beast* castle I'd bought her, and I liked imagining her expression when she got the music box in the mail.

But I couldn't share in her excitement of those things. My interests, like sports and loud music and motorcycles and violent action movies, couldn't be any further from the things she loved.

I simply could not shake this creeping sense of dread in

thinking Wilder would be so much better off with a man like Zeke. And yet she'd turned him down for a commitment-phobic, fumbling idiot who wouldn't know a romantic gesture if it smacked him on the ass.

When I first met Wilder, I made a big deal out of the fact that I wasn't interested in a serious relationship. But after just a few months, I couldn't even envision a future without her. I loved her so damn much, and I knew beyond any shred of doubt that I wanted to spend the rest of my life with her. Hell, I could easily picture *marrying* her, which just a short while ago seemed utterly impossible.

Though I knew she cared for me a lot, I wasn't sure if she loved me. I could easily imagine a happy future with her for *me,* I worried what kind of future it would be for her. All I could think of was the way she looked and sounded at Amanda's wedding. Sad, but determined. She knew what she wanted in a man and refused to settle for less.

It scared me to death that she was in danger of settling for me.

I couldn't keep wasting her time like this. If I wasn't right for her, I needed to let her go so she could find the person she was supposed to be with. It would grind my heart to dust to break up with her, but I loved her enough to let her go if that was what would make her really, truly happy.

It was probably a good thing I had a week-long road trip coming up with the team. That would give me some time to think.

I had the horrible, sinking feeling that by the time I came back, I'd have to leave Wilder for her own good.

24

WILDER

Cam finally came back from his Bay Birds road trip, and my stomach did excited somersaults as I drove toward our favorite brunch spot to meet up with him. A week without him had felt like forever. Even though at times our schedules made it impossible to see each other for a week at a time, knowing I *couldn't* see him made me crazy. How wonderful it would be if we could live together. I'd be so happy to sleep in the same bed with him every night, even if he just slipped under the covers late at night after a ballgame. At least we could spend precious moments together in the early mornings, before life got in the way again.

I kept postponing the inevitable—we were long overdue for The Talk. I didn't require a lifetime commitment from him—not that I wouldn't love that—but I needed some kind of reassurance that he was as serious about me as I was about him.

And I *was* serious about Cam. Sometimes it scared me to think about how serious I was, since I was worried to death that he didn't feel the same. It was strange. Though he never said the words, I got the feeling from his body language and his actions that he cared deeply for me. Simple things, like a look or a touch, told me how he felt. And his sweet gestures, like sending me the Cinderella music box. It showed me he paid attention to my interests, and the song "A Dream is a Wish Your Heart Makes" was absolutely perfect. He knew that because he knew *me*.

I sighed when that very song came up on the Disney station. Cam was so wonderful. I just wish I knew where the hell I stood with him. I'd been with him longer than any other man since Danny, and yet we still hadn't made anything official. I guess Cam liked it that way. Without a formal commitment, he could keep his options open. That was the last thing I wanted—I had no interest in any other options. I only wanted him.

I should just come right out and ask him. He might not want to put a label on our relationship, but I really needed to. I couldn't just be one of his "options" forever. I supposed this morning's brunch was as good a time as any to broach the difficult subject.

I could tell something was off the moment I saw him in the restaurant. There was a sadness in his eyes, and I couldn't fathom why. I'd followed his road trip with the team, and both of his outings on the mound had been good. So good, I'd regretted missing out on post-good-game sex. He was always terrific in bed, but after a good performance at the ballpark, he gave an even better performance in bed.

"Hey," I said when I approached the table.

"Hey." His smile was forced. I was sure of it.

"Are you okay?" I asked.

"Yeah. Sure, I'm fine."

I hesitated for a moment, expecting him to get up and

hug me since we hadn't seen each other in a while. He didn't, so I reluctantly sat down.

"I missed you," I told him.

"I missed you too, Wilder," Cam said, sounding distracted. He didn't really look sad anymore. Just kind of aloof. I often had to wonder what was going on in his mind because he rarely told me, but this time I had no clues from his body language.

We filled our plates at the brunch buffet and sat back down at the table.

"I caught some of your games while you were on the road," I said. "You were amazing out there, Cam."

His face brightened. "Thanks. My two-seamer is really coming along."

"Trace Ridgerton always said you were gonna master that one."

"Yeah, he did always have faith in me. He's a good guy," Cam said.

The conversation lagged, and I became hyper aware of the clinking of dishes and the background noise of other people's conversations while ours stalled. Normally we talked a little about baseball and then he would ask about theater stuff, and somehow we would lose track of time because we enjoyed each other's company. Something was definitely wrong.

A horrible thought occurred to me.

Maybe Cam had slept with another woman while he was away. That was the risk of being in a non-exclusive, non-official relationship. He'd never sworn fidelity to me. And yet I'd hoped he would be faithful anyway. Maybe he was feeling guilty for being with somebody else. Or maybe he was finally getting tired of me, just as I'd feared.

I needed to just ask him what the deal was with us already. Get it over with.

But I couldn't do it. I was too terrified of the answer. How do you ask a question that you really don't want the answer to?

"I got you something," I said, finally breaking the tense silence between us.

"You did?" he asked, his brow furrowing.

"Don't worry. It's nothing big."

Cam had a real thing about me spending money on him. He practically forbade it. He had so much money, and I had so little. He insisted he loved buying stuff for me, and he didn't want me "wasting" my money on him.

I pulled out the small gift from the bag I'd brought.

Cam laughed when he saw his present, and the sound was a relief. Laughter was the reaction I'd expected.

"How ... nice," he said with a chuckle.

I'd bought him a pair of Maryland flag socks, knowing how crazy it made him that everyone in this state seemed obsessed with the flag. Cam still claimed to hate Baltimore, but I thought the place was growing on him, whether he wanted to admit it or not.

"You don't have to actually wear them," I told him with a smile.

"Thank you, Wilder," he said. And there, right there, I saw a glimmer of affection. It gave me a tiny ray of hope that maybe he wasn't done with me yet.

We finished our meal, mostly getting through with small talk. I hated small talk, at least with him. I remembered how long we'd spoken to each other on our first date, how we hadn't wanted the night to end. What had happened to that?

What was happening to us?

25

WILDER

I called an emergency lunch meeting with Amanda. I sure as hell wasn't hungry—I'd just eaten, plus my interaction with Cam this morning made me feel like throwing up. Amanda worked in human resources at a large hospital in Baltimore, so we agreed to meet there. Like an idiot, I'd texted her that I was in crisis. She flipped out, then I explained it was an emotional crisis, not a life-threatening one. Dear friend that she was, she quickly agreed to take an early lunch break and get together ASAP.

I nearly cried when I saw Amanda sitting in the cafeteria waiting for me. It was just such a relief to see her friendly face. I could always count on my dearest friend to be there for me. My family meant well, but lectures on how I was wasting my life with theater were not exactly constructive. My parents knew I was dating Cam, and they were even kind of impressed that I was dating a Baltimore Bay Bird. But they didn't know Cam was stringing me along. If they had, they'd probably tell me I was wasting my time with him.

For once, they were probably right.

But forget them. Amanda would listen and provide advice without being judgmental. She always did.

"Are you okay?" she asked, standing to greet me. At least *she* gave me a hug.

"I guess so," I said wearily. "I mean, not really."

I plopped down into the seat across from her.

"Did you want to grab some lunch first?" Amanda asked.

"No, thanks. Believe me, I'm not hungry."

"What's going on?" Worry shone in her eyes.

"Are *you* okay?" I asked her.

"Yeah, sure. Why?" She looked confused.

"I don't want to just show up here and dump all my problems on you, Amanda. I feel like I'm always doing that."

She smiled softly. She had always been the type of person everyone came to with their problems. Though she genuinely enjoyed helping people—that was why she enjoyed working in human resources—it could be a sore subject for her sometimes. All too often she got lost in the shuffle, and people sometimes forgot she had feelings too. She'd gone through a rough time with Rusty for a while with that very issue. He had gotten much better, thank goodness, and had learned how to take excellent care of her. It was one of many reasons why they were so happy together.

"I appreciate it, Wilder. I'm fine, but I'm worried about you. What's going on?"

"It's nothing new really, I guess. Same old situation with Cam, except now it's getting worse."

"What do you mean?"

"Well, you know I always say he's so difficult to read. When we first met, he was adamant about not wanting to be in a real relationship, and he made sure I knew it. But over time, it kinda felt like he was changing his mind about the whole thing. Tell me the truth, Amanda. Am I crazy for thinking things might be different with me?"

"Of course not. It's possible that he genuinely thought he never wanted to settle down but then felt different when he met the right woman."

"That's what I was hoping. And for a while it really seemed to be the case."

Amanda took a bite of her sandwich, nodding.

"It's hard to explain why I felt that way, but it's the little things, you know? Could be something as simple as the way he looks at me sometimes. That, and he can be so thoughtful."

"Cam does seem to do some really sweet things for you," Amanda agreed. "The music box for one."

"Right?" I said, feeling a tiny surge of hope that maybe all wasn't lost.

"I mean, getting you that castle you always wanted from the Disney Store in New York was generous, too, but the music box was on a whole other level. Like he actually put a lot of thought into finding something special that would cheer you up as opposed to buying something in a store you were already in, if that makes sense."

"It does make sense, but remember, Cam was the one who took me to the Disney Store in the first place because he knew I would love it."

"True," Amanda said. "So what exactly is the problem right now?"

"Okay, this might sound dumb," I said with a weary sigh, unsure how to explain why I was suddenly panicking. "But he just seemed off when I saw him this morning. We haven't seen each other in a week, and I really missed him. Something was definitely wrong, but as usual, he won't talk about it."

"That must be frustrating," Amanda said.

"It's maddening," I said. "Look, I know guys aren't generally great about expressing their emotions, but Cam takes that to a whole new level. It's like come on, give me something here. Give me some kind of clue about what is going on inside your head, dude!"

"What would happen if you just asked him what was wrong?"

"I asked him if he was okay. Of course he said he was fine."

"Of course." Amanda shook her head in annoyance.

"He was just acting so weird," I said sadly. "Amanda, I'm really afraid he might have slept with somebody else while he was on this road trip."

She gasped. "Oh no, do you really think that? How could he do that?"

"As much as it makes me sick to my stomach just thinking about it, do I really have any right to be mad? We never said we were exclusive. That's the problem. What we have together, whatever it is, certainly feels serious to *me*. But what if he doesn't feel the same way? The more I think about it, the crazier this whole thing sounds. Just hearing myself talking about it out loud. I'm basing this whole relationship on what? Because he looks at me a certain way and buys me gifts? What the hell is wrong with me?"

Amanda let out a short, sharp breath. She was uncharacteristically angry, which really took me by surprise.

"What?" I asked, alarmed at her expression.

"I'm just really tired of Cam jerking you around," she said, dropping her sandwich on her plate in annoyance. "I get that he has a hard time talking about his feelings, but enough is enough already. Wilder, ever since we were little girls, we dreamed of meeting the right man. And you deserve nothing less than a guy who is totally devoted to you. If Cam can't be that guy, then he needs to stop wasting your time. He's not the type to settle down? Fine! He can go the hell away and leave you free to find somebody who actually deserves you."

I blinked, shocked by Amanda's outburst.

"Wow," was all I could think of to say.

"One way or another, you need to know exactly where you stand with Cam and what his intentions are."

Sighing heavily, I said, "I guess I know that."

"There's no 'I guess' about it," Amanda shot back. I blinked again.

Leaning toward me across the table, she said firmly, "Wilder Price, you are *nobody's* side piece."

I sucked in a deep breath and slowly let it out. I had never thought of it that way. But Amanda was absolutely right. Sure, it might not technically be cheating if I wasn't officially Cam's girlfriend, but why was I willing to settle for potentially being a part of a harem?

"He's not comfortable talking about his feelings? Too damn bad!" Amanda said, continuing her rant. "He's gonna have to deal with it, at least long enough to tell you the truth about his future plans with you."

"Funny how that doesn't typically bother me all that much. The way he won't talk about what he's feeling. I mean, I agree we have to talk about our relationship. There's no getting around that. It's just crazy how I always thought I wanted some kind of Prince Charming type. A man who was super romantic to sweep me off my feet. Cam is nothing like that, and I'm okay with it. More than okay with it. I think he's wonderful just the way he is."

"But you still need to know where you stand."

I nodded. "I want to know, but ..."

"You're scared to find out," Amanda said. Her tone was gentle now.

"I love him," I whispered.

She smiled sadly. "I know."

I had never actually told her that before, but best friends know these things.

"I'll be here for you no matter what happens," she reassured me.

"I know you will."

I put my head in my hands, fighting back tears. When I finally looked back up at her, I said, "I just don't want to go through what I went through with Danny again. And this will be so much harder."

"Because you love Cam more than you ever loved Danny."

"Exactly," I said, wiping my eyes.

"I'm so sorry you're dealing with all this, Wilder."

"Thank you."

"The best thing to do is to get it over with as soon as possible. Just ask him if he wants to make your relationship official. Or better yet, tell him you don't want to stay in a relationship that's not serious. Let him know that as much as you care for him, a casual fling just isn't for you."

"I will," I said, determined not to wuss out this time. Enough was enough already, and the uncertainty was wearing me out. "Thanks for being there for me, as always. Okay, no more whining from me. Let's talk about you. What's new with you?"

Amanda stared at me for a moment. Then she broke into a grin.

"What already?"

"Wilder, I'm pregnant."

I squealed loud enough to turn every head in the cafeteria. "Are you serious?"

Eyes shining, she nodded.

"That's amazing! I'm so happy for you."

I could hardly believe it. Amanda, my nearest and dearest childhood friend was gonna be a *mom*.

"I know it's awfully soon after we got married, but after what happened with Rusty, we figure life is short. There didn't seem to be any reason to wait because you just never do know what's gonna happen in life."

"Yeah." I nodded, feeling determined. "I know what you mean."

We spent the rest of Amanda's lunch break excitedly talking about the baby, my brain already swirling with ideas about a baby shower. I was so excited about being an aunt.

Amanda's baby news made me even more determined to take charge of my future. I was done waiting around for Cam to make a commitment. I remembered the mental vow I'd taken on the day Rusty and Amanda had taken their marital vows. I had decided I would hold out for the perfect guy who was right for me. And if he never showed up, I'd find my happily ever after on my own.

It was time for an ultimatum.

26

———————

CAM

I'd made up my mind to break up with Wilder, but when I saw her at brunch, I didn't have the balls to do it. One look at her face and every ounce of courage in my body vanished.

Hours later, wandering aimlessly around the field at Old Bay Stadium, lost in thought, I was sure cutting her loose was the right thing to do. The more I thought about it, about us, I couldn't imagine her ever being truly happy with a guy like me. Those words from "I Will Always Love You" seemed tailor-made for me. I wasn't anything like the man Wilder had dreamed of. Not even close. I had to quit being selfish, thinking only of the fact that she made me happier than I'd thought possible.

This wasn't about me. Or at least, it shouldn't be. This was about what was best for Wilder. I needed to set her free so she could find a man who was actually worthy of her.

But how the hell do you break up with a woman when you're in love with her?

I tossed some warm-up pitches with Trace in the bullpen before the game, but my heart just wasn't in it. And he knew it. Trace was my ideal catcher, and we worked perfectly together. I always pitched a better game when he was catching me than with anybody else.

"What's up, man?" he asked, approaching me, baseball in hand. "Don't lose focus now. You're on a hot streak, and for once the Bay Birds got a real shot at the playoffs."

"No pressure," I said grimly, knowing he was right. The Birds were in first place after years of being on a losing streak. Fans were getting excited, as the playoffs were a real possibility.

"What's going on? You've been weird lately," Trace said. "Even for you."

"I'm fine."

"The fuck you are. Spill it."

"It's nothing."

"It's not nothing, so what is it? Girl trouble?"

I held my expression even, or so I thought. Something, I didn't know what, must have given me away.

"I knew it," Trace said with a sigh. "Did you break up with Wilder?"

"Not yet."

Trace's brown eyes opened wide. "But you're going to?"

"Yeah."

"Damn. I didn't see that one coming. Now, if you'd said she broke up with *you* ..." Trace said with a chuckle.

"Dude, same. That wouldn't have been that surprising."

"You don't seem happy about it. So why are you dumping her?"

I winced at those words. I hated the idea of Wilder feeling dumped, but I guess that was accurate.

"I'm not happy about it. But she's better off without me."

Trace laughed. "You're an idiot."

"You don't know what you're talking about," I snapped.

"The hell I don't." He seemed amused at my pain, which made me want to punch him. "You think the two of you are too different, and she can do better than you."

"Don't you think she can do better than me?"

He laughed again. "Well, of course she can. She's a ten. And you're like, I don't know. Whatever this is," he said, grimacing and gesturing at my body.

I chuckled at that.

"Trust me. I'm not good for her."

"Why don't you let Wilder decide what's good for her? She's a grown woman."

"We just don't have anything in common."

"I've seen you together. When you were both running all over New York, you seemed to have plenty in common. You getting bored with her?"

"No!"

"Are you in love with her?"

After a moment, I admitted, "Yes."

"Are you stupid?"

"Probably," I said, this time with no hesitation. "Look, Wilder is just like this touchy-feely, artistic, creative type."

"And you don't like that?"

"Of course I like it. Those are a bunch of things I love about her."

"And we're back to you being an idiot," Trace said, shaking his head.

Now that I was saying these things out loud, I realized maybe he had a point. I wasn't making a lot of sense.

"I just think she'd be better off with a creative theater-type guy than with me."

"Has she ever said that?"

"Well, no."

"Has she ever shown any interest in guys like that since you've been together?"

"I guess not."

"So you're basically saying you're gonna break up with a gorgeous, nice, talented woman because you're being paranoid?"

I didn't have any kind of clever retort to that. Trace was so annoying when he made sense.

"Cam, you fuckin' dumbass, if you're interested in Wilder because of all the ways she's different than you, isn't it possible she feels the same way about you? Would you only be interested in another athlete? Have you ever even dated a softball pitcher?"

"No."

"Are you only interested in women who talk about sports all the time?"

"Okay, okay, I get it. I'm an idiot."

"I think we've established that conclusively, yes," Trace said with a laugh. "If it helps, I never in a million years thought I would end up with Sarah."

"Really?" That shocked me. Those two were perfect together.

"Oh, that's right. You don't know the story."

"What story?"

"The story of when Sarah and I first met."

I shrugged. "I thought you guys met when you were doing charity events for the team or whatever."

Sarah's job on the team had to do with promotions for the Bay Birds and organizing fundraisers and whatnot. Some poor kid with cancer had wanted to meet Trace, kind of like a Make-a-Wish deal, and Sarah had helped arrange it. I thought that was how she and Trace had gotten to know each other. The kid survived, thank God, and had been out of the hospital for a while now. All three of them had kept in touch, which was cool.

"Nope. We met in high school."

"No shit?"

"Oh yeah," Trace said. "Cam, I tortured Sarah in high school. Bullied the hell out of her."

"Damn." I hadn't seen that one coming.

"That was back in Minnesota where we grew up. And the most fucked up part was that when I moved out here, I didn't even recognize her."

"Bet she recognized you."

"Hell yeah, she recognized me," Trace said, and the sorrow that crossed his face took me by surprise. "At first, I couldn't figure out why she was so nice to everybody else and seemed to hate me. After a while, I wore her down and we started dating. Even slept together, and I still didn't remember her from high school."

"Dude," I said.

"I know," he said with a grimace.

"If you're trying to make me feel better about myself, mission accomplished."

Trace laughed. "So happy I could help." Then he grew quiet for a moment. "I really hurt her back then. The shit I did. I was pretty fucked up at the time—messy home life and all—but that's no excuse. I still can't believe how awful I was to her. And now? I would fucking kill for that woman. Can you even begin to imagine how hard it must have been for Sarah to trust me after what I did? But we're inseparable now, and we have this awesome kid together."

There was no doubt in my mind that Trace and Sarah were perfect together. I would never have guessed *that* backstory in a million years. But, knowing what the two of them had overcome to be together gave me hope.

"I never thought I wanted a serious relationship, and now that I do, I'm afraid I'll suck at it."

"People change, Cam. Maybe you are the type to settle down after all, and maybe you'll be damn good at it. You won't know unless you give it a try. I bet you haven't even told her you loved her yet."

Silence from me.

"Quit being a dumbass, stop overthinking shit, and tell Wilder you love her."

I considered my options. Break up with Wilder and make us both miserable, or tell her I love her and spend the rest of my life doing my damnedest to make her happy.

I really was stupid.

The choice wasn't hard.

"I will, Trace. I'll tell her."

"Good. Can we play baseball now?" he asked, sounding like a kid on a sandlot wanting to play with his friend.

I laughed. "Sure, why not?"

We went back to warming up in the bullpen, and my pitching was better than ever. I was nervous as hell about telling Wilder I loved her, but I much preferred that problem over figuring out how to break it off.

The crowd cheered loudly for me when they announced my name as the starting pitcher for the Baltimore Bay Birds. They really were terrific fans, and I had to admit Baltimore did have a unique charm. Even if they were utterly obsessed with putting Old Bay crab seasoning on all their food. Seriously I'd seen Old Bay *ice cream* for God's sake. And of course they put that damned flag everywhere. They certainly had a lot of pride in their city and their state, and lucky for me, that pride extended to their baseball team. As much as I liked to play up my New York toughness sometimes, it was nice not to be hated anymore. Even most of the guys on the team had warmed up a bit to me.

Throughout the game, I thought a lot about how and when I would say those three little words to Wilder. I didn't want to screw up something so important, but I'd never said "I love you" to a woman before. I wanted to do it right. Though I still wasn't the lovey-dovey type, she deserved some romance from me.

I was really in the zone tonight, calm for the first time in a long time knowing maybe I could finally make Wilder mine. My two-seamer was kicking ass tonight, which was such a thrill. About time I'd gotten that pitch right.

Then I slowly realized what everybody had been careful not to point out to me, lest they jinx it.

Five innings in, and I had a perfect game going.

27

WILDER

You're nobody's side piece.

Amanda's words still echoed in my ears as I stood on the college stage, indulging in a little vocal therapy. Sometimes it took a best friend who had your best interests at heart to tell you the harsh truth. She was right about me and Cam. I loved him so much, and the idea of being without him was torture. But then, the idea of Cam being with other women was also torture.

Since when was I the type of woman willing to share her man with somebody else? I was disappointed in myself for letting this go on so long. I really didn't blame Cam since we'd never made anything official. I blamed myself for not making *my* intentions clear from the beginning. And my intentions were to either find a man who could be faithful or find happiness on my own.

If Cam couldn't be that man, I would have to let him go. No matter how much it hurt.

I'd spent the evening belting out songs that gave me courage, including "I'd Rather Be Me" from *Mean Girls* and "Where Did the Rock Go" from *School of Rock*. Songs about the empowerment of being yourself. Then, just for fun, I sang "History of Wrong Guys" from *Kinky Boots.*

Singing had its usual therapeutic effect, and I felt stronger by the minute. I wasn't looking forward to my upcoming frank discussion with Cam, especially considering our last awful brunch date. I didn't foresee things going well. Still, times like these when I felt super connected to my art, I knew I could survive just about anything.

When I took a quick break to grab some water, I saw a text from Amanda. She wanted me to come over to Power Bar and Grill. It was sweet of her, but I really wasn't up to it, and I told her so.

Please?? She texted back. *We really want you here.*

I sighed heavily. I was so not in the mood to hang out at a bar right now. Being here and singing onstage had made me feel so much better. Hanging around a bunch of people would just drag me down. And yet Amanda was always ready to drop everything when I needed her. I owed her no less. If she wanted to hang out for a while, it was the least I could do. I wondered if maybe her sisters were there and they were celebrating her pregnancy announcement.

Okay. I'll be right over.

I was surprised when she texted back: *Hurry.*

Now I was worried. I hoped everything was all right. Gathering my stuff, I left as quickly as I could.

It took forever to find a damned parking spot downtown. That shouldn't have surprised me considering the Bay Birds were playing. My mind went wild with everything that could be wrong for Amanda to need me right away. The horrible thought crossed my mind that something was wrong with the baby, but then I realized she would hardly hang out at the bar if that were the case. She'd have been at home with Rusty, not at his work. It was just so unlike her to send an emergency text. Me? I was the drama queen. I did stuff like that all the time.

Finally, I made it to the bar.

"Wilder!" Amanda called out the second she caught sight of me across the unusually busy bar. It was a Wednesday, and they didn't even have trivia or karaoke going on.

I rushed through the crowd to where Amanda had thankfully saved me a seat at the bar.

"Sweetheart, don't jinx it," Rusty said to Amanda, his blue eyes wide.

"What the hell is going on around here?" I asked.

"Have you checked the sports news lately?" Amanda asked.

"No." My blood ran cold.

Oh God. Cam's been hurt.

Horrible visions of him being struck in the head by a batted ball filled my brain.

"He's got ... something going on in the game," Amanda said, glancing at Rusty. She seemed nervous, keyed up, but not upset necessarily. I calmed down enough to finally put the pieces together. The crowd gathered at the sports bar. Rusty's words about not jinxing it.

"Oh my God!" I said, finally catching on. "Is it ... well, is it the thing that sometimes happens with pitchers in the majors, like maybe once or twice a season? Or is it the thing that almost never happens?"

"The thing that almost never happens," Amanda said, clapping her hands together.

Though a pitcher having a no-hitter was exciting and awesome, the other thing was much more unusual. Sure enough, I looked up at one of the many televisions on the wall and saw the scroll at the bottom of the Bay Birds game broadcast.

"Cam Becker has a perfect game going through eight innings."

I gasped, feeling weak in the knees. Fumbling, I took a seat on the barstool. An incredibly rare feat in baseball, a perfect game meant the pitcher didn't allow anyone to get on base at all during the entire game. No hits, no walks, no hit by pitches. *Perfect pitching.*

I covered my mouth with my hands as I stared at the television, and I felt Amanda's supportive hand on my back. Watching Cam try to get the last few outs to hold onto his perfect game would be torture. I wished I could be there for him at the stadium, not that it would do him any good. I was probably better off here with a bunch of supportive Bay Bird fans.

He made it through the eighth inning, and that's when I started tearing up.

"I know, I know," Amanda said, rubbing my shoulders from her seat next to me. "It's wonderful, but it's awful."

"Exactly," I said, wiping my eyes.

I wanted this so desperately for Cam. What made it even harder was that I knew exactly what he was feeling right now. The same way I'd felt about my big audition and was waiting for the results.

And I remembered all too well how devastated I was when I didn't get the part.

Oh God, I don't want him to go through that.

Cam had worked so damn hard to get to this point. I thought about his pain when he was traded from Atlanta, and I cringed recalling his reaction to his terrible outing on the mound in New York of all places. This was his big chance to show them all what he was made of.

I drew in several deep breaths as we waited through the commercial breaks in the game. Though Cam had already proved he was a masterful pitcher with tonight's performance, I hoped with all my heart he could close the deal and make it to the record books. I drew in another shaky breath just thinking about it.

Amanda heard it and squeezed my shoulders again. This was excruciating for me; I couldn't imagine what Cam was going through.

At last, we'd made it to the top of the ninth with the Bay Birds up 3-0. If Cam managed to hold on to the perfect game, or even if he simply didn't allow anyone to score, there would be no need for a bottom of the ninth.

I was glad I hadn't been watching this game from the beginning. I didn't think my heart could take it.

Shaking my head in wonder, I watched Cam's unbelievable performance up on the screen. To think, so far he'd dispatched twenty-four hitters.

Terrified, I watched his first windup of the ninth inning. The pressure on him must have been unbearable, not to mention the high pitch count. There was a reason managers rarely left starting pitchers in past the seventh inning or so. Fatigue had set in by then.

Everyone in the bar got quiet, their rapt attention on the game.

Cam popped up the first batter, the type of ball everyone assumed would be caught by one of the outfielders under normal circumstances. But these were far from normal circumstances. The right fielder caught the ball, thank God.

One down, two to go.

Using that incredible two-seamer pitch he was becoming famous for, Cam expertly struck out the next guy.

One to go.

I didn't think I was gonna make it. I'd never felt such terror in my life.

Cam would be okay if this didn't happen for him. It wasn't as if he would lose his job over it or anything. But having a perfect game was such an incredible, career-defining feat. And I wanted him to have this dream come true more than I'd wanted anything in my entire life.

Please, please, please.

The potentially last batter of the game hit the ball. *Hard.* Everyone in the bar collectively gasped. I was pretty sure my heart stopped. It was a hard ground ball to short. Brady scooped up the baseball, and the camera followed it as it sailed over to the first baseman. Everyone held their breath. The ball hit the glove of the first baseman a second before the batter reached the base.

Cam Becker's place in baseball history was secured.

The entire bar exploded into screams, whistles, and applause. I broke down and *wept,* my head in my hands.

He did it, he did it, he did it.

When I remembered how to breathe normally again, I recovered enough to join the celebration. Amanda and I held each other and cried tears of joy.

28

CAM

I damn near fell to my knees on the mound in sheer relief.

I could have kissed Jacob "Smitty" Smith at first base for catching the final out. I hardly had time to wrap my head around what I'd just done, not with my entire team charging the field, headed right toward me. The guys mobbed me, and I got so many slaps on the back that it hurt.

I was in heaven.

Never in my life had I even dared to dream such a thing could happen. A perfect game had always seemed so far out of reach that it wasn't even worth thinking about. All I ever wanted was to be a good pitcher, but this? This was unimaginable.

But it was actually happening.

I did my best to soak in the moment and be grateful. As humble as I wanted to be, I couldn't help thinking the Atlanta Suns could *suck it*. I hoped they were filled to the brim with deep remorse for letting me go. May they forever be known as the team who cut loose a pitcher who went on to have a perfect game that very season.

Okay. Enough with the mental *I told you so*. Much better to focus on the positive.

The crowd was going berserk, and it was fucking wild.

Wilder.

I wondered if she had seen any of the game. She always tried to tune in when she could, but I didn't remember if she had work or rehearsal or whatever tonight. All I knew was I wanted to share this with her as soon as humanly possible. None of this would feel real until I shared it with her.

After things had settled down and I'd had a few minutes to catch my breath, I gave a few on-field interviews. I told everyone who pushed a microphone in my face that it had been a team effort, and I truly meant it.

"A perfect game is a lot more than just pitching," I told the woman from *The Baltimore Bugle*. "It can't happen without top-notch defense, which we sure as hell have. And no matter how many guys you get out, you can't have a win without run support. An incredible team with incredible hometown fans—that's what made this happen today."

Eventually, I made my way to the showers and got cleaned up. I checked my phone to find lots of congratulatory messages. Though I didn't see anything from Wilder, Rusty texted me.

Dude!! Unbelievable!! Helluva party going on over here at Power if you want to join us. If my pretty face isn't enough to get you to come, Wilder's here. Maybe you can get her to stop crying, lol. I think she was more stressed out over those last few innings than you were.

So Wilder had seen the game. I could just imagine her tense expression as she stared at the television. I could hardly wait to get to her so we could share this triumph.

Heading over now. Thanks, man, I texted back.

Hyped up, I was tempted to speed recklessly down the

highway on my motorcycle. But reason prevailed—I wanted to make headlines as the guy who had a perfect game, not the jerk who managed to get himself killed on the way to his own victory party. Besides, picturing Wilder's face made me want to act responsibly.

Finding parking was easy now that the baseball crowd had gone home. I took a moment to stop and gaze out at the Chesapeake Bay in Baltimore Harborplace. Everything had been such a blur, and yet I wanted to remember every second of this incredible night.

Taking a moment to be grateful for everything I had was incredibly calming. And I had a lot. Once I made Wilder mine, I really would have it all. I just hoped like hell she wanted me.

The whole place burst into applause the moment I walked in. Clearly, Rusty had told them I was coming. I waved as modestly as I could, resisting the urge to pump my fist in the air. Then I quickly scanned the room, searching for Wilder. I caught sight of her at the bar. Our eyes locked, and it was like something out of a movie.

Oh God, my heart.

Not only had I been totally out of my mind for even thinking of breaking up with her, I'd been crazy to think I could have gone through with it if I'd tried.

Wilder Price was the love of my life, and I couldn't wait to tell her that.

29

WILDER

As I stared at Cam from across the crowded room, I could hardly believe what I was seeing. And yet there it was.

The Look.

My breath caught in my throat as Cam gazed at me with that all-important tender expression filled with desire and affection and devotion. After years of being leered at by men staring at my chest and legs like I was a piece of meat, I had nearly lost faith that anyone would ever look at me like that. But there was no mistaking what I saw on Cam's face. He was gazing at me the way Rusty gazed at Amanda, like he couldn't imagine life without her.

My rational mind knew at least part of it could be due to the natural high of his incredible athletic achievement; my emotional heart told me there was much more to it than that. My knees went weak as we stared into each other's eyes as if there was no one else in the room. In that moment, Cam didn't have to tell me he loved me. I already knew.

This was exactly what I couldn't articulate to Amanda. The way Cam showed his devotion through his looks and actions but never with words. His love was crystal clear to me now.

Cam made his way through the crowd, and I jumped off the stool. He grabbed hold of me, and we wrapped our arms around each other. I held him tight. No words were necessary. He knew that *I* knew how important tonight was and what it meant to him.

When he let go of me, he tenderly stroked my cheek. "Rusty warned me you couldn't stop crying."

Laughing softly, I shook my head. I hadn't even realized my tears had started up again.

"I think I'm still recovering from an attack of high blood pressure. Oh my God, Cam, that ninth inning ... I didn't think I was gonna get through it. I can't imagine what you were going through."

"I know it was rough, but I'm glad you got to see it," he said.

"Me too."

Whatever had upset him the other day at brunch, he seemed to be over it. I was still worried that maybe he'd slept with someone else and he'd been feeling guilty about it. Perhaps it was just one of those things he had to get out of his system before realizing he wanted to be with me. As convinced as I was now that he loved me, we still needed to have that all-important talk. We still needed to get our relationship sorted out once and for all. Though I didn't need a big dramatic declaration of love, I did need a solid and *verbal* promise that he'd be faithful. But not tonight. This was Cam's moment, and there was no way in hell I'd take it away from him.

To their credit, the Baltimore Bay Bird fans who had gathered kept a respectful distance while Cam and I hugged each other and spoke privately for a few moments.

But they were waiting for a chance to interact with their hero.

"Feel like signing a few hundred autographs?" I asked him, turning to face the crowd.

"Sure, why not?" he said with a chuckle. "Not like my hand is tired or anything."

I nodded sympathetically and watched as he interacted with the fans, giving each one at least a few seconds of attention before moving on to the next. We would be here for a while, but that was fine with me. I was so proud of him.

After he'd greeted and signed for just about everybody, he took a moment to address the crowd.

"Ah, I just want to thank everyone for coming out tonight. Thanks for supporting the team, not just on the exciting nights like tonight, but also when we sucked."

Cam got a laugh from the crowd.

"I know, um ... I know I wasn't exactly gracious when I first got to town," he confessed.

There were some nods from the bar patrons who clearly remembered what he'd said about Baltimore when he was traded to the Bay Birds.

"But I wanna say I really appreciate the way all you Bay Birds fans have embraced me. And, as much as I hate to admit it ..." He pulled up a nearby chair and plopped his leg down on it. "I think I'm slowly becoming one of you."

With that, he pulled up his pants leg to reveal the Maryland flag socks I had bought for him. The crowd went crazy, laughing and clapping for him. Cam grinned and rolled his pants leg back down.

I wondered if he'd been wearing the socks during the game, like a good luck charm. Probably not, since the team likely had strict uniform rules. Anyway, it didn't matter. I felt honored that he was wearing the gift I'd given him, and he had certainly endeared himself to the Bay Birds fans in the bar.

Rusty came over to talk to Cam when the line of fans had finally dissipated.

"Thanks so much for coming here tonight, dude," Rusty said with a grin, clearly thrilled with the turnout. "It's definitely the most popular bar in all of Baltimore right now."

"My pleasure," Cam said with a smile that was slightly sad. After a moment, he added, "I wish you could have been there tonight, man. That last out ... that could have been you."

My heart sank at those words. It hadn't occurred to me that the final out of Cam's perfect game had been caught by the first baseman. If not for Rusty's life-threatening heart condition, he would have been on first base.

"Yeah." Rusty nodded. "I know. But still ... this?" He scanned the bar still filled with customers despite the late hour on a weeknight. "This is exactly what I envisioned when I opened this place," he said, his deep blue eyes filled with gratitude. "A bunch of Baltimore baseball fans coming together and experiencing big moments in the game together. As a community. Helps keep me connected to the game even if I can't play anymore."

"That's pretty cool," Cam said.

It was tough not to start crying again, but somehow I managed. Cam wrapped his arms around me, and we just stood together for a while. Rusty went over to talk with Amanda. He tenderly rubbed her belly, and they shared a happy smile.

"Amanda ..." Cam said. "Is she ..."

"Yeah," I said happily. "She just told me this morning."

"Wow, that's great."

"I'm not sure how many people know yet, though," I said.

"Got it. Don't mention it to Brady Keaton or the whole world will know in five minutes."

I laughed. "Exactly."

Brady was a sweetheart, but he tended to be excitable. I doubted secret-keeping was his strong point.

Pretty soon, it was last call. By law, bars in Baltimore had to close at 2am at the latest. Otherwise, the party might have kept going all night.

"Wanna go back to my place?" Cam murmured in my ear. "You know how I get after a big win."

The thrill of deep, sexual desire tingled between my legs. We hadn't had sex since he'd gotten home from his road trip. And yes, I knew how he was after a big win. And this was the biggest win a pitcher could get.

"Yes, let's go. *Now.*"

People cheered for us as we headed out. It felt like we were a couple headed off on our honeymoon.

Might as well have been, because Cam was about to rock my world in bed.

30

CAM

"Cam, Cam, Cam!" Wilder cried out from underneath me as I got the headboard rattling like never before. "Oh God!"

She arched her back, allowing me to penetrate her even deeper. It drove me wild when she kept screaming my name. It felt like all of Baltimore would know I was as good in bed as I was on the mound. I'd never felt more confident in my life, and I loved that Wilder could be the beneficiary of all my excess sexual energy.

Wilder screamed for me not to stop, but I had to if I wanted to give her the most pleasurable experience possible. Sure, banging the hell out of her felt great, but she needed more to come hard. I pulled out of her, and she gasped. She didn't complain because she knew what I had in mind.

Lying on her back, she positioned herself with her knees up and legs open. That was her favorite position when I went down on her. I tongued her, and she screamed my name again. Then she got quieter. She was close.

"Oh Cam," she panted. "Don't stop ... Oh God ... don't ...

don't you dare ... st—" She threw her head back and cried out my name over and over again.

I usually gave her time to catch her breath before ramming into her, but I just couldn't. I slammed into her hard, and she grabbed the back of the headboard.

"Oh God, you're an *animal*, Cam." Her deeply satisfied and sultry tone told me it was a compliment.

I grunted and growled as I came, sure as hell sounding like an animal.

Exhausted as hell from the late night and our athletic sex, we fell asleep in no time.

Unfortunately, I had to head out early the next morning. The Bay Birds had a bunch of interviews they wanted me to do. Though I hated to wake Wilder, slipping out while she was still asleep would have been worse.

"So sorry I have to go," I told her, kissing her gently on the mouth.

"Wish you could stay," she said groggily. "But I know your public needs you."

She smiled sleepily at me, and I knew she understood.

"Get some rest," I said.

And I damn near added "I love you." It seemed so natural in that moment. Thank God I didn't say it. Telling her for the first time was a huge deal, and saying it after sex and sleep was a terrible idea. I wanted to make the whole experience much more romantic for her. She deserved that for putting up with me.

After I wrapped up a bunch of interviews—and damn, it was hard to come up with new responses to the same questions over and over—I texted Rusty to see if he was available. I needed advice on women.

Gross. Not something I ever thought I would need, but it was true. I knew nothing about women when it came to relationships, and I needed some guidance. Rusty texted back, saying I could come over to his place. Amanda was at work, so we would have some privacy. Good thing, because I didn't need an audience for such an undoubtedly awkward conversation.

"Well, well, well," Rusty said as he cracked open a beer and handed it to me. "Of all people, Cam Becker needs advice about the ladies."

As we sat on his back porch, I took a long pull of beer. Rusty was not gonna make this easy on me. And honestly? I couldn't blame him. Not in the least.

"So what's going on with Wilder?" he asked, his eyes filled with amusement. He was going to bust my balls. But he would also help me. I was sure of it.

"Well, the thing is ... I need to ... I just need to figure out how to ..."

Rusty chuckled.

Holy fuck. If it was this hard to talk to Rusty, how in the hell was I supposed to talk to Wilder?

"I see the way you look at her. You're in love with her. Now who's a pussy?"

I took in a terse breath through my nose and let it out. Again, I couldn't blame him if I tried. I had totally called him a pussy for loving Amanda. I had it and probably a lot more coming.

"You do love her, right?" Rusty asked, his tone no longer mocking. He was a nice guy. Always had been. I should have known he wouldn't make fun of me for long.

Dropping my head, I said, "Yeah, I love her."

"You're gonna have to make eye contact with her when you tell her, you know."

"I know." I looked up, panicked. "And what's more, I can't just *tell* her."

"What do you mean?" he asked, casually sipping his beer. I was jealous that he was already safely established in his relationship with Amanda. The hard part was over for him.

"Wilder deserves something like ... I don't know ... big and splashy and, like a big deal and all that. Damn, you wouldn't think sports players could ever be like that, but I keep thinking of how Matt Jovey proposed."

Rusty snorted. "Yeah. Tough act to follow."

Matt, our second baseman, had proposed to Julia on the field in front of thousands of fans. His now-wife was the head groundskeeper for the Baltimore Bay Birds, so his romantic gesture was perfect.

"What about you? You proposed in public."

"Yeah, I did," Rusty said with a cocky grin.

Of course, Rusty's proposal was perfect, too. Wilder had been there. She and Amanda were so close and, as pretty as Amanda was, she was no match for Wilder who turned heads everywhere they went. For years, men had ignored poor, sweet Amanda and it had really hurt her feelings after a while. That was why Rusty deliberately got down on one knee and proposed in a bar after sending a free drink Amanda's way, like so many men had done for Wilder all those years. It was a really sweet proposal.

Damn him.

"Wait, are you thinking of proposing?" Rusty asked, lowering the beer bottle from his lips.

"No, no. Not yet anyway. I mean, I do want to marry her."

"Really?"

"Yeah." I found myself smiling just thinking about it. Never thought I'd see the day, and yet here we were. "But not yet. I know it's too soon. Way too soon. The first step is telling Wilder I love her."

Rusty shrugged. "So do it."

"It's not that easy. How did you tell Amanda?"

"Oh, I haven't told her yet."

"Funny. Real funny. You probably sprinkled the bed with rose petals and wrote her a love poem."

"No, I did it with skywriting."

He sounded so serious that I believed him for a second.

Cackling, he said, "Dude. It's not that complicated."

Rusty paused for a second, then smiled. "Honestly, it wasn't a huge thing when I told Amanda. I mean, saying 'I love you' is a big thing, but that doesn't mean it has to be some elaborate production. Ever since my heart scare, Amanda worries about me. A lot. And when I told her I was buying a motorcycle, I could tell she was upset. It's not that I like seeing her upset, but it meant a lot that she cared so much, you know?"

I nodded. Yeah. I knew.

"So in that moment it just felt like the right time, so I told her I loved her."

"And?"

"And she said it back. Then we had sex."

"Nice," I said, fist-bumping him.

"Cam, just tell her you love her. That's all you have to do."

I wanted to believe him, but his advice just didn't feel right to me. "This is Wilder. You know she's the super dreamy romantic type."

"True," Rusty admitted. "But you're not. And she's with you anyway. Three little words, Cam. You can do it."

"Thanks. And hey," I said, lifting my beer bottle toward his. "Congrats on the baby, man."

He grinned proudly, and we clinked bottles to toast his upcoming bundle of joy.

Rusty was right—I needed to tell Wilder I loved her already, but he was wrong about keeping it simple. Wilder loved all that gooey, lovey-dovey crap, so I needed to do something super romantic when I told her.

Something big.

31

CAM

I spent all the next morning and afternoon practicing my big surprise for Wilder. The Bay Birds had the day off, so it felt like now or never. That, and if I hesitated at all, I would surely lose my nerve. All I said was I wanted to see her, so she invited me to her place. I almost texted that we needed to talk, but then I realized how scary that sounded. That was breakup talk, which was the opposite of what I was going for. I managed to stop myself from screwing that part up, but I'd have to see how the rest of the day went.

"Hi," Wilder said, smiling sweetly when she answered the door.

Already I was overwhelmed by her. She was beautiful as always, wearing a delicate blue blouse that brought out the color of her eyes. But Wilder was so much more than pretty. When I looked at her, I saw the woman who always had my back. The one who put up with my moodiness and laughed at my dumb jokes. The strong, independent lady who tackled an unforgiving industry despite zero support from her family.

I damn near said I loved her right then and there, but I reminded myself I needed to stick to the plan.

"I—I just needed to talk to you," I stammered, my confidence wavering already. Yet I was determined. I could do this. For Wilder.

"Okay," she said, her expression falling. "Is everything all right?"

I realized I'd just said a different version of "we need to talk."

"Yes, yes! Everything is fine. Perfect. Great!" I insisted.

She nodded, looking understandably confused.

I walked into her house, closing the door behind me. Rubbing my chin, it occurred to me that I wasn't really sure how to start. I'd worked hard to memorize a song, but now that it was time to sing it for her, I didn't know how to do it.

This was even scarier than I'd imagined, and I'd worked myself into quite a panic several times already. Why was this so hard? In all those stupid musicals of hers, the guy just burst into song out of nowhere. Turned out it wasn't so easy in real life.

"Dammit!" I burst out suddenly, startling Wilder. "I left the goddamn roses in the car."

"What?"

"Roses. I bought you a dozen roses. You know, like they give you when you're the star of a show on opening night? I was supposed to bring them in with me."

I must have looked and sounded every bit as flustered as I felt because Wilder asked, "Cam, are you okay?"

Sighing, I said wearily, "Fuck, I am screwing this whole thing up."

"Screwing what whole thing up?"

"I can't be a Disney prince!" I shouted.

Wilder's eyes flew open and she stared at me. Then she

laughed softly, gazing at me with a mixture of amusement and confusion, but also with affection. She wasn't laughing *at* me. She was just trying to figure out why I seemed to be having a mental breakdown.

I sank down onto the couch in defeat. "I can't believe how badly I fucked this all up."

"Cam," she said gently. "Why don't you just tell me what's on your mind? And why are you talking about Disney princes?"

I growled in frustration, which only made Wilder laugh again.

"Rusty told me to keep it simple. I guess he was right."

Wilder looked at me, still waiting for me to explain myself.

"I'm sorry I'm such a damn mess all the time. I don't know. I'm just trying to figure out a way to tell you I want to marry you and—"

"*Marry* me?" Wilder cried out, eyes wide. "I wasn't even sure you wanted to be in an exclusive relationship. You've never even called me your girlfriend. Last I heard, you didn't want to be in a serious relationship."

"Oh, I changed my mind about that a long time ago. Guess I never actually said that out loud, huh?"

Wilder slowly shook her head.

"How can you even talk about marrying me? Cam, you haven't even said you loved me yet."

"I love you, Wilder."

Damn. That was easier than I thought.

"That's a good start," she said, sitting down on the couch beside me. "I love you too, Cam."

I sighed heavily. "This really isn't how I planned to tell you."

"What do you mean?"

"At Amanda's wedding, I overheard you talking about looking for your Prince Charming."

"So you thought you had to act like a Disney prince to win me over?"

"Well, yeah," I said, rubbing my forehead. "I mean, not just from what you said, but I know you. You love all that Disney and musical romancy stuff. That's why I was gonna ..."

I suddenly felt embarrassed, not wanting to admit what I had planned to do.

"Tell me, Cam. What were you gonna do for me?"

Wilder looked at me expectantly, and I knew I owed her the truth.

"I got a bunch of roses and I sorta memorized a song from a musical that I was gonna sing for you."

I couldn't even begin to imagine where Matt Jovey had gotten the balls to propose on the baseball field. If the guys on the team ever got wind of what I'd had in mind, I'd probably die of humiliation.

"Wow," she said softly.

"I could still do it, you know. I could—"

"No, no. Cam, you don't have to do anything like that. It's just not your style. And that's okay. I love you just the way you are."

Relief swept through me. I still felt like I was letting her down by not giving her the fairy tale ending she deserved, but it turned out I just didn't have it in me.

"Now about this marriage thing ..." Wilder said, treading carefully.

"Wilder, I didn't mean to blurt that out."

"Oh."

"No, no, no. I mean, I do want to marry you. Someday. I know we're not ready yet."

She nodded. "I do want to marry you. But ..."

My heart sank into my shoes.

"But ..." I said, terrified to hear the rest.

Her eyes filled with tears. "I want to be your wife some-day. But I'm scared." She nearly whispered that last part, and the fear on her face tore my heart to bits.

"Why?"

"Something happened ... Amanda is literally the only person who knows about it."

"My God, what happened?"

Wilder seemed traumatized, and it was killing me.

"I'd been dating this guy for a long time," she said, her voice weary. "And then he proposed to me."

I nodded, afraid to find out what happened next.

"He proposed in the afternoon, and that very night I caught him having sex with another woman in our bed."

"Are you fucking serious?"

Wilder nodded tearfully. "I suppose it's a blessing that I never got the chance to announce our engagement. I just told everybody we broke up. Only Amanda knows what really happened."

"No wonder you seemed so sad at the wedding."

She looked at me quizzically.

"I couldn't take my eyes off you that day."

She smiled sadly, and I could practically read her mind. She thought I'd been staring at her just because she was pretty. To be fair, that was the case at first. It seemed so long ago, and I loved her for a million other reasons now. I wished I had the right words to explain it to her.

"He got bored with me, and sometimes I'm afraid you will too," Wilder told me before breaking down in fresh tears.

"Oh, sweetheart," I said, pulling her into my arms. "I could never, ever get bored with you."

"Attraction eventually wears off," she said bitterly. "Always does. In the end, being pretty can be a bad thing."

"Do you really think your beauty is the only thing I love about you?" I asked, stroking her hair.

"I can't help worrying sometimes."

Lifting her chin gently so I could look at her, I said, "When I first saw you, not at the wedding but at Amanda's bachelorette party at Power, I planned to try to get you in bed."

"Is that so?" she asked in a teasing tone. She knew I was going somewhere with this.

"Then I overheard what you said at the wedding, about wanting a serious relationship and waiting for your prince and all that, so I abandoned the idea of sleeping with you. You seemed pretty vulnerable, and I knew you wanted a real boyfriend, so my plan was to move on to somebody else. Pick up another bridesmaid or lonely girl at the wedding."

"Did you?" she asked, wiping her eyes with a tissue.

"No. I forgot all about that once I heard you sing."

"Really?"

"Hell yeah. Wilder, at first, I thought of you as just a sexy woman with an incredible body. When I heard you sing at the wedding, I don't know—it was like after that I couldn't stop thinking about you. I tried for, like, weeks, but I couldn't. Then I searched up your singing videos because I wanted to hear more of your voice."

Wilder smiled, seeming much calmer now.

"Everywhere I went, every song I heard was suddenly about you. I was attracted to you at first because of your looks, but I fell in love with you for, you know, *you.*"

Though I still wasn't exactly smooth with words, she seemed to understand what I was trying to say.

"If it makes you feel any better, I'm scared too," I told her.

"Really?"

"Yeah. About a lot of things. I'm scared to death that I'm the wrong kind of guy for you."

"How can you say that?"

"Easy. I'm the total opposite of you. I'm the least romantic guy on the planet, and I never know what to do or say. I must sound like an idiot to you half the time."

Wilder seemed confused by my statement, which made me feel a lot better. Her expression told me she didn't feel that way at all.

"So funny you think that. Because I always feel like you always know the *right* thing to say."

"No fucking way," I said bluntly, pretty much proving my point.

Wilder picked up her purse from the floor and rifled through it. She picked out a small piece of paper from her wallet and handed it to me.

It said "Give 'em hell, Belle."

"You texted that to me on the day of my audition. I loved that you had so much confidence in me that you called me by the character's name. It was just so *sweet*. So I took a screenshot and printed it out. I look at it sometimes when I need a boost of confidence."

I was completely blown away. All this time I'd felt so stupid for sending her that text.

"What else are you scared of?" she asked.

"I dunno. I guess I worry I'm too rough around the edges for you. I have a bad temper sometimes. Just like my dad.

My parents were always screaming at each other, which of course scared me off marriage."

Wilder nodded with understanding.

"I worry about my anger issues. Can't help thinking that theater guys like Zeke would never have punched some guy out in a bar the way I did. I acted like such a punk."

"Oh, Cam," Wilder said dreamily. "I swear, normally I don't condone violence, but that was the most romantic thing anyone has ever done for me."

"Yeah?"

"Yes," she said, stroking my cheek. "You defended my honor, Cam. Like a white knight.

"Damn. I never thought of it that way before."

Laughing, she said, "I think we need to get better when it comes to communicating. Seems like we have a lot of misunderstanding going on."

"Sure does. Mostly my fault. I'm not good at talking things out."

"I know that. And for the most part, it's okay. But I can't have you going around thinking I'm disappointed in you because you're not serenading me in the woods like Prince Charming. And I need to be better about telling you what I'm thinking and feeling, too."

"Sounds good to me."

"So, we may not exactly be engaged yet," Wilder said. "But I guess we're, like, official now?"

"As official as a game that's completed five innings. Or four and a half if the home team is ahead."

Wilder laughed affectionately, and I realized she always did that when I said something weird. She seemed to think it was cute. Lucky for me.

"I want to marry you, Cam. But it's best for both of us if we don't rush into anything like that. Between my broken engagement and your parents' bad marriage, I think we both need more time to get comfortable with the idea."

"Agreed," I said. I had zero qualms about spending the rest of my life with Wilder, but the idea of marriage was still a little unnerving. I would have no problem being faithful to her, but the idea that someday we could grow to hate each other scared the hell out of me. Yes. More time would be good for both of us.

"And when we feel the time is right, that's when we'll get engaged," she said, her eyes shining.

Gazing into her eyes had me tempted to throw all rational thinking out the window and propose after all. But reason prevailed.

"Okay," I said.

"When we're ready, I don't need anything fancy. You'll ask and I'll say yes."

"You sure you don't want some big romantic proposal like what Matt and Rusty did?"

"Of course not," she said with deep tenderness in her voice. "Do you know how Brady Keaton proposed to Lyric?"

"No. I don't."

I couldn't imagine what crazy thing Brady had concocted. I was almost afraid to find out.

"He and Lyric were hanging out watching television in their living room and he proposed."

"That's it?" I asked.

"That's it. The two of them really enjoy having quiet time together when he finally gets a break from baseball and she gets a breather from the hospital. Lyric told me that Brady said the moment had just felt right."

"Wow. And Lyric wasn't disappointed?"

Smiling, Wilder shook her head. "She told me it was perfect."

She pulled me close and kissed me, and I growled deep in my throat.

"Hmm," she said, pulling away.

"What?"

"Did you ever stop to consider ... maybe you're not supposed to be Prince Charming? Maybe you're *The Beast*."

The Beast.

I fucking loved that.

"The Beast," I said. "That does have a nice ring to it. I much prefer it to the idea of prancing around in tights like a Disney prince."

A throat cleared. "Umm, is it safe to come in now?"

I closed my eyes in embarrassment. Wilder's roommate was home, and who knew how much of my fumbling she'd overheard. She definitely caught the part about the tights.

"Sorry, sorry," Kerry said as she hurried into the living room. "I hate to interrupt, but I gotta get to work."

"No problem, Ker," Wilder said.

Glancing at me, Kerry said, "You got yourself a keeper there."

"I know," Wilder said.

"Congrats on the perfect game, Cam. That was badass."

Her comment made me feel a lot better, like she wasn't judging me based on whatever parts of our conversation she'd heard.

"Thanks," I said.

"Catch you guys later," Kerry said as she hurried off.

"So," Wilder said. "Since we are as official as a fifth inning ballgame now, I feel like we should do something to seal the deal."

"I think that's an excellent idea."

"Take me to the bedroom, you sexy beast."

Oh yeah. I liked that nickname more by the minute.

32

WILDER

Sex with Cam was better than ever now that we were exclusive. No matter how many women he might have had in the past, I was his present and future. It was still scary to put my trust in another man, but Cam was worth it. I knew in my heart he would never betray me the way Danny had.

"Oh, Cam," I said in a sultry voice after he'd satisfied me once again. "You really are a Beast."

He chuckled, but I got the feeling he really liked when I called him that. I hoped it showed him how much I loved him exactly the way he was. Once upon a time, I thought I did want a deeply romantic type of guy, but it turned out I was wrong. Cam was everything I never knew I wanted.

As we lay naked in bed, Cam held me in his arms. He murmured in my ear, and it took me a moment to realize what he was saying.

He was reciting the words to "Evermore" from the *Beauty and the Beast* musical. It must have been the song he had planned to sing to me. Cam knew every single word.

I gasped softly and closed my eyes as I listened. Each

word was so beautiful because it came from him. I really didn't want him to feel pressure to do anything he wasn't comfortable with, but this gesture was incredibly thoughtful.

"That was so lovely, Cam," I said, turning to face him when he finished. "You really didn't have to do that."

"I wanted to. For you."

"Thank you." I kissed him softly.

"Believe me, you really don't want to hear me sing it."

I giggled and snuggled closer to him.

"Oh, damn," he said.

"What?"

"Those roses are still in the car."

I shrugged. "I'll make potpourri."

Cam laughed. "Always looking on the bright side, you are."

"I try," I said. "Can I ask you something?"

"Sure."

"Did you really go to Rusty for advice on what to say to me?"

"Yeah, I did."

"That's sweet." I could just see them sitting together and talking, Cam bumbling through the conversation and Rusty giving him advice while gently teasing him. That was the kind of adorable relationship those two had.

"I also talked to Trace about what to do."

"You did?" Okay, that took me by surprise. Trace Ridgerton didn't strike me as the type of guy to talk romance with another guy.

"Yep."

"And what did he say?"

"He told me I was being an idiot."

"Aww. Why would he say that?"

"Because I was gonna break up with you."

I shot bolt upright, still stark naked. "You were gonna break up with me?"

"Technically, yes. Hear me out, Wilder. I was only gonna end things because I worried I was holding you back from finding somebody better. I know it's dumb, but when I saw you and Zeke in that show together, and then I found out he'd asked you out and you said no because of me, I ... I don't know. I was just worried about you. And scared to death I wasn't good enough for you."

"Oh, Cam," I said sadly. All this time I'd been frustrated that he wouldn't tell me what was on his mind, and now I realized he'd been stressing out over so many things.

"So after the show, I figured I would think things over while I was on the road, and the only answer I kept coming up with was that you'd be better off without me. So I was gonna break up with you, you know, so you could be free. But then when I saw you at brunch that day, I just couldn't do it."

"Ohhhh," I said, finally understanding everything. "That's why you were so cold and distant that day. I thought maybe you'd slept with another woman while you were away."

Cam's eyes flew open wide in horror. "What? No! Sweetheart, how could you think I would do such a thing?"

"Because we weren't exclusive, so it wouldn't technically be cheating."

"Wilder, I've barely looked at any other woman since we met, let alone slept with one."

"That does make me feel better," I said, lying back down next to him.

He ran his fingers through my hair, soothing and

comforting me. "Damn, we really do need to get better at talking about things."

"We sure do. I would have asked if you wanted to be exclusive that day, but I was really scared of the answer."

"I get that." Turning to face me in bed, he said, "I want to ask you something. Don't worry, I'm not proposing. Yet."

I giggled.

"What do you think about coming to live with me in New York? At least during the off-season. We could still keep your place here for the baseball season if you want."

"Wow, move to New York?"

"Only if you want to. I know you have a job here, but you don't seem particularly attached to it. I'm sure you could find a new job there, and you'd be more available for Broadway and off-Broadway auditions and stuff like that."

A bolt of excitement shot through me.

"Cam, I would *love* to live in New York with you! And not just for the auditions, you know. The idea of waking up every day with you makes me so happy."

"Me too," he said with a smile.

I squealed giddily, which made him laugh. Cuddling up close to him, my stomach tingled with excitement about our future together.

33

WILDER

I sat in the stands with Lyric and Sarah as we watched the Baltimore Bay Birds try to make the playoffs for the first time in years. Though not quite as stressful as watching Cam's perfect game, it was still pretty rough. It had all come down to the last game of the regular season, which made for good drama for the fans but was hard on the girl-friends and wives of the players. No doubt Julia was just as tense somewhere close to the field where she could watch Matt play. Amanda and Rusty were holding down the fort at Power and watching the game with lots of fans.

Two runners on, two outs, and the Bay Birds were down by one in the ninth inning. This was it. Their last chance to win or at least tie the game.

"Oh God, not again," Lyric said, holding her hand over her heart as Brady stepped into the batter's box.

When Brady played for the Richmond Dominoes, he'd made the final out that had ended the team's playoff hopes. He had done nothing wrong; after all, someone had to be the last out of the season. Lyric had been watching the game in Baltimore and seeing Brady's pain had nearly wrecked her.

I put my arm around her shoulder and squeezed her for support. I knew exactly what she was going through.

Cam had been the starting pitcher with Trace catching. He'd had a no-hitter going through the third, but then he'd given up a couple of runs. Not a bad outing at all, but they'd taken him out of the game in the fifth. Watching the game was still excruciating, even though his part was done, because I knew how badly he wanted to make the playoffs.

All too soon, the count was 3-2 on Brady. Why did *every-thing* have to come down to the last second like this?

Lyric began tearing up, and I wished I could do something to help. She closed her eyes, unable to watch, so I kept an eye out for her.

"Ball four! A walk!" I told her.

"Oh, thank God," she said, letting out her breath and wiping her eyes. Like being the doctor she was, being a baseball wife was also not for the faint of heart.

Before we knew it, Matt hit a double, sending two runners home and ending the game.

We all went crazy, screaming and hugging each other. The entire stadium erupted in thunderous yelling. I could just imagine the scene right now at Power, excited Bay Bird fans all yelling at the TV and high fiving each other. One of the most beautiful things about sports was the way it brought the community together. In a moment like this, there were no politics or any other divisive differences. Right now, we all celebrated like one happy family.

The energy from the crowd was so much like the energy I felt onstage when performing for a full house.

I loved that.

34

CAM

The Bay Birds had a good run this year. We made it to the playoffs, which thrilled the fans and generated new interest from them after years and years of having a losing team. The Bay Birds got knocked out of the playoffs on the road, but I was still really proud of everything we'd accomplished.

When our flight from California arrived in Baltimore, there were signs all over the airport thanking the Bay Birds for a great season. I think it made all of us feel better about having to come home until next year. Already, it was hard to remember a time when I hated Baltimore. Like New York, the city had its bad side for sure. But it also had its cute and charming quirks. I used to think their slogan "Charm City" was some kind of ironic joke, but now I realized it was pretty accurate. Baltimore would never replace my hometown, but it wasn't a bad place to be.

On the shuttle ride back to the airport parking lot, I scanned the sports news on my phone and grinned when I saw a mention of me that included my new nickname. Before we left for Cali, a sports reporter asked if I had a nickname like Brady "The Crusher" Keaton did. I shrugged and said, "Well, my girlfriend calls me The Beast."

And that was how I became Cam "The Beast" Becker.

Wilder got a huge kick out of that. She saw the interview on TV and called me right after to tell me how much she loved that I'd mentioned it. I got the feeling she also loved that I'd said on live TV that I had a girlfriend, making it clear I was unavailable.

And, contrary to what I'd thought my whole life, I was thrilled to be exclusive, official, and unavailable to any other woman.

God, I loved Wilder.

And I loved Baltimore.

THANK you so much for reading the fifth book in The Boys of Baltimore Series.

Heartfelt thanks to you for reading!